Courtesy of Duval County

Tacarra

Urban Dynasty Presents

ISBN-13: 9788326190703
ISBN-10: 1477123456

Cover design by: Art Painter
Library of Congress Control Number: 2018675309
Printed in the United States of America

Contents

Synopsis

"You have a collect call from...Shariq."

After recently relocating to Duval, Jenelle realizes the only thing that has changed is her surroundings. That was until she missed a call from an unknown number. When the caller calls again... she answered, not knowing that she was answering her destiny.

Shariq got caught up in the wrong place at the wrong my time, sending him to the last place he wanted or needed to be. When he tries to call home, his call is intercepted by an unfamiliar female.

Intrigued by the sensual voice, he embarks on something that could be beneficial for the both of them.

Follow Shariq and Janelle on their journey to love during and after lockup.

Chapter One

Shariq "Frost" Carter

"Fuck," I grunted as I watched Jas let my dick disappear down her throat. I was supposed to be at my mama's house for the lil' cookout she was having. It was nothing special, but in Duval, we didn't need a reason. It was Friday, and the sun was out...so were we.

I was concentrating on the nut that was building as Jas did her thing. My ringing phone was breaking my concentration and pissing me off at the same damn time. I refused to answer it until I emptied my nuts down Jas' throat, though.

"Get ready, shorty," I warned, just as I palmed the back of her head and shot all my seeds down her throat. Once I was drained, I released her head, and she got up off of her knees while I caught my breath. My phone started ringing again, and I saw that it was my mama.

"Ma, I'm on the way," I said as soon as the call connected.

"Shariq, hurry yo' ass up! These niggas fuckin' up my meat and I ain't got time for that bullshit today. Hurry yo' ass up!" My mama fussed into the phone.

"I said I'm on the way, Ma. Chill out."

"I got yo' chill out," she said, hanging up on me. Laughing, I got up and headed toward the bathroom that was connected to my room. I was already in the process of getting dressed when Jas called, asking could she come over. As I was preparing to take a shower, Jas walked in.

"Can I join you?" she asked. I assessed her body from top to bottom and contemplated on taking her up on her offer. Looking at her five foot five frame, I contemplated bending her thick chocolate ass over, but I didn't have time.

"I wouldn't mind, shorty, but I need to get to my mama's house. I'll hit you up when I leave there, though," I offered. I would've invited her, but my mama couldn't stand her ass. I was chilling in the yard one day with this other shorty and Jas popped up and started fighting. Ever since then, my mama ain't have shit for her ass.

"Your mama still mad at me?" she asked.

"Shorty, my mama hates your guts." Wasn't no need to beat around the bush. That's one thing that I didn't do—spare feelings.

I watched as she sauntered back out of the bathroom and went inside the shower to wash up real quick. Once I was finished, I got dressed in a simple white tank top with some camouflaged cargo shorts and a fresh pair of white forces. I put my two Cuban link chains on and my Movado Heritage watch with the green face. I had small gold hoops in my ears that I never took out. After spraying on my signature cologne, *Y by YSL*, I was good to go. Jas had already let herself out so all I had to do was grab my keys, phone, and wallet. On the way out, I grabbed a white towel to throw across my shoulder because I knew I was going to need it in all this damn heat.

The ride from my house to my mama's on the Southside took about thirty minutes from my house out near the beach. When I pulled up, the block was already packed, and kids were running around all over the place. When I got out of my car, my daughter, Shariah, ran right to me.

"Daddy!" she squealed, jumping into my arms.

"Wassup, baby girl?" I kissed her temple as I placed her back on her feet. She was eleven going on twelve, but she was still my baby. "Your mama dropped you off?"

"Yes, sir. She said that she would be back later to pick me up."

Nodding, I walked through the yard, dapping people up along the way until I made it to the back, where I found my mama fussing and cussing at my uncle Ray. That nigga swore he was a grill master and couldn't even season the meat properly.

"Nigga, get yo' ass out the way," I said as I approached him and my mama.

"Thank God, somebody with a lil' bit of sense showed up before all of my meat got ruined. This nigga here swears he knows what he's doing and already burned a slab of my good ribs. Move yo' ass, Ray." I watched as she playfully shoved him in the back. Ray was my mama's baby brother. They were close, just like me and my sister, Shadai, were. Speaking of, I didn't see her around.

"Ma, where Shay at?" I asked.

"She ran to the store to get more ribs and some ice," she informed.

I nodded at her information before I turned my attention toward Ray. "Nigga, move yo' non-cooking ass out the way. Let a real nigga show you how this shit is done." I talked my shit as Ray moved from in front of the grill.

"You acting just like yo' nappy headed ass mama. Y'all some hating ass niggas," he joked.

"Nah, you just a muthafucka that can't cook." I smirked, checking the meat that was already on the grill. "Ma, go get me that sauce from out the kitchen that I keep in there. This shit looks dry as fuck." I laughed.

"Fuck you, nephew," Ray retorted.

"Nah, nigga. Fuck this chicken."

I started doctoring the chicken up and the ribs that weren't ruined. Shadai finally showed back up, and she had her nigga, Alonzo, with. He was alright. He was a square ass nigga that tried to act like he was

5

from the hood. That nigga was from Mandarin—the white part.

"I'm glad I didn't have to depend on you to bring the food because we would starve," I joked as she walked up.

"Whatever nigga. I had to go pick my nigga up," she voiced. I looked at her when she said that because the fuck she picking that nigga up for?

"'Sup, Zo. Where yo' car at?" I asked.

"I had to put it in the shop this morning. I can't get a rental until tomorrow. You know I wouldn't have Shay out here just chauffeuring me around," he explained. I just looked at him blankly instead of offering a response.

"Shay, take that meat to Ma so she can clean and season it for me. Bring a pan on your way back out, too." My sister left and Zo stayed back and chopped it up with a nigga. Like I said, I didn't have a problem with him. I just wanted to make sure he wasn't playing with my sister.

After I got the food on, I grabbed a beer and headed back to the front to see what was happening out there. When I got there, I saw that more niggas had pulled up, even my homie, Cruz.

"Wassup, my boy?" I slapped hands with Cruz as I approached him.

"Ain't shit. This muthafucka packed as hell, ain't it?"

"You know it. Niggas find out that free food and drinks are involved, and they pile out like roaches. Ain't bringing shit but an appetite." We shared a laugh, and I took the pack of blunts out of my pocket and lit one of the pre-rolls. After taking a strong pull, I passed it to Cruz.

"What took you so long to get here?" I asked.

He blew the smoke out of his mouth before responding. "I pulled up on this lil' chick before I pulled up. You know how that shit goes."

"Hell yeah. Jas dropped through before I got here. That's what took me so long and Ray fucked up the ribs." We shared a laugh before he passed the blunt back to me.

"You went to holla at Boogie?" I asked.

"Shit, I forgot. I can go after we leave here," he offered.

I was annoyed by his slackness, but I brushed it off…as usual.

"Don't worry about it. I'll go when I leave here. Just meet me at my spot in the morning."

"Nah, you don't have to do that. I'll still go."

"I said I got it. Just be at my house in the morning to pick the shit up." He silently agreed, and we continued to bullshit around. It was close to ten o'clock when I saw Mariah pull up to get our daughter. At this point, she could've let her stay, but she was funny acting, and I didn't have time for her bullshit tonight.

"I hope you didn't have my baby 'round none of your lil' hoes," she said as soon as she walked up, popping her fuckin' tongue with every word she said. I couldn't stand that ratchet shit, but it's too late to complain now.

"Man, MaMa, chill out. Ain't no bitch been here. She's been playing with her friends and cousins since she's been here."

"Uhm hmm. Where my baby at?"

"In the house. Where else would she be this late at night?" I asked with a scowl.

"Boy, please. That girl is practically grown. That's her problem now; you baby her too much." Instead of responding, I ignored her ass and let her walk off.

"I'on see how you do it, bruh," Cruz pointed out.

"I don't," was my response.

Shadai and her boyfriend came out and left right before Mariah came back out with my baby girl in tow. She came and hugged me before asking could she come stay with me tomorrow. After assuring her she could, I kissed her cheek and watched as her ratchet ass mama took her home.

"You about to head out?" Cruz asked.

"Yeah, I need to go get this pack and take my ass to sleep."

"I'm about to head out, too, but not without getting a to-go plate first." He smirked.

"Greedy ass, nigga, but I feel you." We both got up and headed inside. My mama was already fixing plates to go, and she was piling them up too. After I handled my business and showered. I was going to smoke and smash that shit.

"Aight, Ma. I'm out. Make sure you lock up." I pulled her into my side and kissed the side of her head.

"I am. You know I'm about to fall through the bed. I've been up since six o'clock this morning. Let me know when you get home," she said.

"I will."

After making sure my mama locked up, I got in my car and headed toward my plug's spot. I already told him that I was coming through later, after I found out that Cruz didn't go. When I pulled up to his house, and pulled into the garage. Muthafuckas were nosy as hell, and he didn't play that shit. People only assumed what the fuck was going on, but they didn't have any solid proof.

"What's good wit' ya?" he asked.

Boogie was a good dude and has been my plug for years. I got in the game at sixteen and I didn't fuck with nobody but him. Even when his prices went up, I paid that shit.

"Ain't shit. I ain't mean to stop by your shit this late, but Cruz was supposed to get the shit, but he claimed he forgot," I explained.

"I figured it was some shit with him when you hit me up. I prefer dealing with you, anyway. I know that's ya mans and all, but I don't trust that nigga. You need to watch out for him too," he said.

"Nah, he's straight. He just doesn't think sometimes."

"That's your call. Don't say I didn't warn you." He went in the back and came back with my duffle bag full of Molly and Coke. I sold weed too, but this was my primary source of income, hence the nickname Frost. I dapped him up and was on my way. While I was headed home, Jas hit my phone.

"Wassup?" I answered.

"You still at your mama's?" she asked.

"Nah, I'm headed home now. You tryna let a nigga slide through?"

"Do you even have to ask?"

Smirking, I responded, "Nah. I'll be there after I go home and shower."

"I'll be waiting." We ended the call, and I lit my blunt as I cruised 295 to get home. When I got off of my exit, I turned to go to the gas station for blunts instead of going straight home. When I turned, I saw two JSO cars ducked off. I prayed that they didn't fuck with a nigga tonight and left me alone. That prayer didn't even leave my mouth good before I saw blue lights behind me.

"Fuck!" I cursed to myself. This shit couldn't be happening to me right now. I had a pound of Molly and Coke in the trunk, and an unregistered gun inside of the armrest. As a convicted felon, I knew I fucked up with the gun. I just hoped that they didn't search the trunk. I had the shit in a hidden compartment, but that didn't mean shit to them. They would find any reason to fuck with a nigga. I pulled into the store parking lot so I could have witnesses if those muthafuckas tried some shady shit.

"Get out the fuckin' car!" One of the officers yelled.

Slowly, I got out of the vehicle and had my hands raised so that they could see them.

"Step away from the vehicle," the older officer said.

Doing as I was told, I walked away from my car with my hands on my head. While one officer walked over to the car, the other came toward me and placed my hands behind my back to cuff me.

"Do you know why we stopped you?" The officer cuffing me asked.

"Nah, I don't." I tried to keep my temper at bay but inside my blood was boiling.

"Your back taillight is out," he informed.

"Can't you just give me a ticket for that and let me go?"

11

"We could, but after running your tag, we have probable cause to search your vehicle." He smirked, but I kept my comment to myself. I watched intensely as I watched the other officer search through my car. I had a blunt in the ashtray and my personal stash of weed in the armrest, along with the gun. I was currently on probation, so I knew they were about to take my black ass back to jail.

"Are you aware that you have marijuana and a gun inside of your armrest?" I looked at him like he was stupid because that was a dumb ass question. Of course, I knew that shit. It was my fuckin' car. Instead of responding, I invoked my right to remain silent because I knew that shit was next.

I listened as the officer read me my rights and silently cursed myself for not taking my ass straight home. The only good thing about this was that they didn't go through the trunk and find that duffle bag. That shit would've given me football numbers, and I didn't have that kind of fuckin' time to give no-fuckin-body.

Once we got to the jail and they processed me, I was finally able to make a phone call. I called my mama first, and she didn't answer. Knowing her, she took a sleeping pill and didn't hear the phone ringing. I was going to try Shadai next, but I couldn't remember her phone number for shit. She made me sick, always changing her shit like she was running from the Feds. The first number I called for her, a nigga answered the phone. It didn't sound like Zo, so I hung up. I tried wrecking my brain for a few more minutes before they started tripping over the phone. Finally, thinking I had the right number, I dialed it and listened to it ring in my ear.

"Answer the fuckin' phone, Shay," I said to myself.

When I heard the generic voicemail come on, that only repeated the number I dialed, I got pissed all over again, but I still decided to leave a message.

"Shay, it's me. I got stopped on the way home and I was dirty. I know I ain't going to court until Monday so call E and be up here with her." I left the message and hung up. Blowing out a frustrated breath, I let them take me to my cell, where I would spend the next forty-eight hours until I was able to see a judge.

This was able to be one long ass weekend.

Chapter Two

Jenelle "Nellie" Calloway

I have been in Duval for a little over a month and so far I don't have any complaints. I did my research before moving here and knew which parts to stay away from. I ended up renting a condo on the Southside for me and my ten-year-old son, Kyren, and I loved it. The neighborhood was quiet and close to everything. My neighbors minded their business just like I minded mine.

I moved here because, for one, the clientele was great, and I was ready for a change. One of my regulars that found me on Instagram lived here. She made a trip to Savannah once a month to get her nails done by me. She even referred a few clients. She was the one that made the suggestion that I move here to gain more clients that couldn't travel. My Savannah clients weren't happy, but I had a few that let me know that they'll travel to the ends of the Earth with me before they let somebody else touch their hands. Like now, I was servicing one of my Savannah clients, Michelle. I've been doing her nails since I started five years ago. I was almost done with her shaping, so it was time that I started with her design.

"Shell, you know what we're doing today?" I asked as I made sure her XL stiletto nails were on point.

"Nii, why would I know that?" She smirked. "You know I let you do whatever you want to my hands, and you won't hear not one complaint from me." She was telling the truth. I was just holding conversation when I asked what we were doing because I already had an idea in mind. I saw a pink marble and chrome design that I ran across on Pinterest that I was going to recreate and add my own touches to it. By the time I was done, you'd never know that it was a recreation.

"You know I got you, girl. Sit back and let me do what I do." I pulled out my brushes and colored acrylic and began my process. I studied each nail carefully to make sure that I didn't leave any room for error.

"Nellie, you found any good niggas out here yet? You know what they say about these Duval niggas, and I need to know from somebody if it's true before I come and snatch one of 'em up." I looked up at her and noticed the smirk on her face that I knew was a mimic of the one I wore.

"Chy, I haven't had any time to do much of anything but get my house together and make sure that Kyren adjusts well," I stated honestly.

"Well, you need to get out this house and into

these streets. You can even bring Kyren to my mama for her to watch him, and I'll go out with you. Just let me know and we can make it happen." She offered. I nodded to let her know that I understood her and concentrated back on her hands. By the time I was done an hour later, she was satisfied and so was I. Shell was my last client of the day and I was going to relax and probably take Kyren out to Urban Air later. He hasn't met any friends since school hasn't started yet, so I made sure that he didn't get bored just sitting around the house and playing his game all the time.

After I was done, she paid me via Zelle, and gathered her things to leave but not before promising me to make an arrangement to go out when she came for her next appointment.

After Michelle left, I cleaned up the room that I used for my nail studio before going into Kyren's room to check on him. When I got in there, he was playing his video game with my best friend, Alexis' son, Alex.

"Nigga, watch out!" he yelled.

"Dooda!" I fussed.

"My bad, Ma." He gave me that award-winning smile looking like his ugly ass daddy.

"I'm done for the day. When you're done with your game, we're going to go to Urban Air. Okay?" It took him a minute to concentrate on what I was saying because he was so focused on his game.

"Ky!" I called him again.

"Huh?" he responded.

"I said we're going to go to Urban Air when you get off the game with Alex."

"Okay, Ma," he responded, not even looking at me.

Shaking my head, I left his room and went down the hallway and crossed through the living room to go into my room. When I got inside, I walked through my small hallway that was inside the room. That was the one feature I loved. I was like my room was a small apartment inside of my condo. Walking into my walk-in closet, I searched the hangers for something to wear to the trampoline park. I wasn't doing any jumping, but I was going to be comfortable. It was nice out today, so I decided on wearing a cute graphic t-shirt set with the matching tan tights from SHEIN. Picking out a pair of tan Jordan 4s, my outfit choice was complete. I went and prepared for my shower, but not before tying my short pixie cut down so that it wouldn't curl up in the shower.

It took me all of an hour to get myself together and dressed before I went to check on Kyren. When I walked inside of his room, he was finally taking his headset off.

"I'm done. We're about to go?" he asked.

"In a few. Go clean up your mess and go wash up." I watched him go put his controllers and

17

other toys up before going into his drawer to get clean underclothes and socks before going into the bathroom that was inside of his room. That was another reason I loved my condo. Kyren had his own bathroom as well. His room was not as big as mine, but it was big enough for his bunk beds.

While he did that, I called my best friend Alexis. I hadn't talked to her yesterday, and we never missed a day.

"Wassup, bitch?" she answered.

"Nothing, much. Those boys of ours just got off of the game and now I'm waiting on Ky to get dressed so we can go to Urban Air. We'll probably go to Applebee's or somewhere afterwards because I know I won't be cooking when we get back." I took a pull from my weed pen as I sat back and talked to Lex and waited for Ky. I smoked weed, but I didn't want to really smell like it or burn my damn nails, so I reduced my smoking to pens. I used an online vendor, so I never worried about running out.

"That sounds like a plan. If I didn't have to work this weekend, we could've come down, but we'll plan something real soon because I miss y'all already."

"We really do. Definitely before the boys go back to school. We can plan a back to school trip for them, or something." I suggested.

"We definitely can. I'll be looking, too."

"Sounds like a plan. Jarvis done came crawling

back yet?" I asked about her baby daddy. When we talked earlier this week, she threw him out because another random chick called her, saying that she was messing with him, too. That's a cycle with them and I hate that for my friend, but I'm going to be her friend and not her critic. That's the problem with most females these days. They're quick to tell their friends how dumb they are and they're sitting next to her, being dumber. That ain't in me. If my friend says fuck that nigga today, we gon' say fuck that nigga. If she decides she wants to marry him the next; we're going to pick out colors. That's their business...not mine.

"Girl, I blocked his ass, but tell me why this nigga sent me a stack on Cash App and in the note section he said, 'that hoe lying'. I nicely transferred it to my account and still kept him on the block list. Fuck him and that Shrek and Donkey looking bitch." I choked on the smoke coming from my pen because this girl was ignorant as hell.

"Wait, bitch." I coughed through my laughter. "Shrek *and* Donkey?" I was still laughing because I could picture an ogre looking bitch with a donkey face.

"Shrek and Donkey, bitch. But fuck him and her hunchback ass." We shared another laugh and continued to hold conversation before Kyren walked out stating he was ready. My son was so handsome and was my lil' twin. He looked fly in his camouflaged outfit that I got from SHEIN. He picked out his dark green Jordan 4's to match and had his locks pulled up in a ponytail, showing off his faded sides. I got his ears pierced when he was three, so he had his studs in and his lil' gold chain with a child-sized 'K' pendant on.

"Okay, Ky. I see you." I smirked as he dusted off the imaginary dust from his fit.

"You see me?" he retorted with a smirk.

"You ready?" I asked.

"Yes ma'am. I called my dad and told him you were taking me out and he sent me some money on Cash App," he stated.

"That was good. Keep it. It's my treat." I smiled as I got up to slip my shoes on. After grabbing my purse and phone, I escorted Kyren outside to the car. I also liked the fact that the garage was attached to the front of the building, so I didn't have to worry about a parking space or getting wet when it was raining. After making sure Ky was buckled up in the backseat, I pulled out of the garage and headed the short distance to the trampoline park. When we arrived, I was glad that it wasn't too packed. I parked, then waited for Ky to get out and we strolled into the building with him right by my side.

After getting our tickets, I purchased his slip resistant socks and let him do his thing until he worked up an appetite. That took about two hours before he came running to me, saying that he was ready to go. I was glad because I was good and hungry myself. Making sure he had his shoes tied, we were out the door and headed to get some food.

As we sat and waited for the server to bring out our food, I decided to make small talk with my son.

"So, how do you like it here so far?" I asked.

Shrugging, he said, "it's alright." My baby sounded sad, and I knew it was because he missed his friends.

"It'll get better once school starts. Maybe we can go to a gym or park close by the house to see if you can make friends that way. You'd like that?" I asked, and he nodded. I gave him a small, reassuring smile in return.

The server finally returned with our food, and we enjoyed it before heading back home. When we got back home, he wanted to play his game with Alex, and I allowed it since they didn't have school the next morning. While he went into his room and played his game, I went into mine and took a quick shower. Afterwards, I tied my hair down and slipped on my bonnet before retrieving my phone so I could scroll through social media before I dozed off to sleep. As I was scrolling, I saw that I had a missed call and a voicemail. I knew absolutely nobody here outside of a few clients. The missed call could've been a potential client, so I listened to the voicemail first before calling back. When the message started playing, I scrunched my face up because I was confused as to why I would be getting a call like this.

"You have a collect call from…Shariq." I heard the operator say. "Your call will automatically be connected," she continued. I had it set up like that because my baby daddy found his self in more trouble than I care to admit. But this wasn't him. This was someone named, Shariq and I had no clue as to why he was calling me, but my nosy ass listened to the message, anyway.

"Shay, it's me. I got stopped on the way home and I was dirty. I know I ain't going to court until Monday so call E and be up be here with her." The call ended, and I was just as confused as I was when I first listened. I did feel bad for whoever this was, though. It was a Friday night, and I knew for a fact that he would be there, at least until Monday. That sucked, but there was nothing I could do but shrug my shoulders and go back to being nosy on The Shade Room and Hollywood Unlocked. Those two sites were my weaknesses, and I indulged several times a day with not an ounce of shame.

The next morning I woke up, I handled my hygiene and fixed me and Kyren breakfast before my first appointment came at eleven. As I did that, my phone rang. Looking at the display, I saw that it was the number from last night. I looked at the phone as it rang and stopped. They must've hung up. That was short-lived because not even a minute later, they called again. This time, I answered.

"Hello?"

Chapter Three
Shariq

I spent the night in the county and was ready to get the fuck out of here, but I needed to get in touch with Shadai. I thought to call my mama again, but she was only going to fuss and right now I didn't need to hear that shit. I needed to get in touch with Shadai so she could get things in order for me.

After they did the morning count, I went straight to the phones and picked up the first available one and tried Shadai again. The phone rang, and no one answered.

"Pick up the fuckin' phone, Shay," I growled.

Picking up the phone again, I dialed the number again and this time someone answered, but the voice I heard didn't belong to my sister.

"Hello?" the husky, yet feminine voice answered.

"Who is this?" I asked.

"You called me, so who are you looking for?" She shot back. I wanted to curse her ass out, but clearly I wasn't going to be able to get in touch with Shadai by myself, so I changed my tone.

"My bad, shorty. My name is Shariq. As you can tell, I'm in a jam and I was trying to reach my sister. Her ass can't keep a number a hot minute, so I don't know her number by heart. Can you do me a solid and contact her for me?" I asked, hoping she agreed.

"Uhm, how would I do that? You don't know her number and I don't know her name. Oh wait. What's her name? I'll look her up on Facebook or Instagram." She offered, completely catching me off guard. It was rare that complete strangers volunteered to help you.

"I really appreciate you looking out shorty," I said.

"Janelle," she stated firmly.

"My bad, Janelle," I emphasized. "Her name is *Just Shadai* on Facebook and *yeahitsshay* on Instagram." I rattled off the information to Janelle.

"I'll call her since we're not friends. She may not get the message." I agreed.

"Aight. I'm gon' hang up and call you back in a minute," I informed, and she obliged. As I hung up the phone, I prayed that Shadai answered and didn't blank out on that damn girl. I waited approximately a whole minute and called right back. The operator went through her spiel. Then I heard her voice.

"Hello?" she answered.

"Did you get her?" I asked anxiously.

"Yes, she's still on the line. Let me merge the call." She clicked the line and the next voice I heard was Shadai.

"Shay?" I called out.

"Damn it, Riq. What happened?" She asked as soon as she heard my voice.

"Man," I drawled, rubbing my hand over my hair. "You need to stop changing yo' damn number," I fussed.

"Boy, if you'on tell me why you're locked up, you gon' know something." Shadai was older than me and swore she was my damn mama.

"Give me your number so I can write it down. I don't want to keep tying up shorty's line like this."

"Janelle," she corrected.

"My bad. *Janelle*."

I listened to my sister rattle off her number and we both thanked Janelle before she hung up and I called my sister right back.

"What the hell happened, Shariq?" she interrogated as soon as the call connected.

"Muthafuckas pulled me over as soon as I got off the highway. They searched my shit and found my gun and my stash," I stated. Shadai knew not to say much over the phone, but she knew it was more to the story.

"That's all?" she asked.

"Yeah. I know they impounded my car, but I

25

need you to holla at Cruz so he can go pick it up. I also need you to hit my lawyer up so she can have her ass down here. I know they're about to be on some dumb shit and I don't need to be blindsided."

"Anything else?" she asked.

"Go pick up Riah for me. She asked could come to my house and as you can see, that's impossible. You can let her mama know what's going on but let her know that ain't shit changing with my arrangements with my daughter." Mariah would try that bullshit and say my people couldn't get my daughter and then Shadai would beat her ass and still get my daughter. Nobody liked her ass, including me.

"I got you, baby brother. Anything else you need me to do before Monday?"

"Yeah, send ol' girl that called you something for looking out," I stated.

"Shariq," she called my name, but I ignored her tone.

"Can you just do that Shadai and not ask questions?"

"Uhm...hmm," she agreed.

The operator interrupted, letting us know that we only had thirty seconds left on the call.

"I love you, Riq and I'll be there on Monday," she informed.

"I love you too, Shay." The call disconnected

after that, and I went back to my cell to take a damn nap. My head was starting to hurt, and I needed to lie down before that shit got worse.

When I woke up from my nap, Janelle was on my mind heavily. I don't know if it was because she genuinely sounded like she wanted to help me or because she sounded fine as fuck. Either way, I found my way, heading towards the phone and dialing her number.

"Hello?" she answered, sounding unsure.

"What's up, baby girl?" I greeted.

"Janelle," she corrected. I could fuck with it.

"My bad, Janelle. I just wanted to call you back and thank you for helping me get in touch with my sister. You don't know how much that shit meant to me. Did you get what she sent you?" I asked. Since we had her number, it was easy to send her a stack via Apple Pay.

"I did, and you didn't have to do that. I tried sending it back, but she refused the refund." I laughed because Shadai knew I didn't want that money back.

"She did right because I wanted to thank you and that's the only way I knew how," I revealed honestly.

"Thank you, Shariq."

"You got it. What you doing?" I found myself asking.

"Uhm...I'm in the middle of working on my client," she informed.

"Word? What you do, shorty?" I noticed this time she didn't correct me.

"I do nails," she stated.

"That's what's up. Maybe you can hook me up with a manicure or some shit." I teased.

"I got you. What you want, a French tip or a freehand design?" she asked.

"I hope you're talking to your client because if not, you got me fucked up, shorty. But check it. I just wanted to call back and say thank you for looking out. I don't know how I would've gotten in touch with my people if it wasn't for you."

"You're welcome," she responded.

The operator came on the line and let us know that the call only had thirty seconds left and I couldn't lie...I felt some kind of way. Instead of expressing it, I thanked her again and let her go on about her business, but this wasn't going to be the last of our encounters.

My day went by smoothly. It was a few people from the hood that I fucked with that were in here, so shit was somewhat normal. As about as normal as normal could be.

It was around three o'clock when I heard one of the guards call my name.

"Carter!" he called out.

Looking up, I saw Douglas standing in front of the open cell. He was one of the homies from the hood, so I knew my stay here would be smooth.

"Your lawyer is here," he informed. This was the visit I was waiting on, letting me know that Shadai got on her shit. I got up and stretched before I followed Douglas to one of the small meeting rooms that were reserved for lawyers. When I got inside, I saw my lawyer, Erielle Johnson, sitting at the table with a pair of glasses sitting on the bridge of her nose as she looked through the folder that was set in front of her. I knew Erielle from around the hood, but she got out and did some shit with her life. When she came back to the city, I immediately had her on retainer. I knew I needed a lawyer, so why not get one that I was acquainted with.

"What's up, E?" I greeted her as I sat down.

"Hey, Shariq," she countered.

"What you got for me?" I asked, over the small talk.

"Well, Shariq. This is not going to be easy. You just got out of jail six months ago. You're a convicted felon that was caught with a gun and marijuana. The best I can do is get you a bond, and depending on the judge, that could be hard," she explained. It wasn't shit I wanted to hear, but I knew it would be a hard case and being a black man, they didn't give a fuck. I'm not blaming them, but damn...give a nigga a break.

"In other words, I have to wait until Monday to see what my fate is?"

"That's exactly what I'm saying, but you know that I'm going to do all that I can to help you out."

"I know, E and I appreciate it." She got up, and I hugged her before Douglas came and escorted me back to my cell. I was going to take my black ass to sleep and when I woke up, hopefully it would be Monday.

Chapter Four

Janelle

It's been two days since I heard from Shariq, and I hated to admit that I wanted to talk to him again. It was crazy that I was lusting after a man that I didn't even know. After snooping on Shadai's social media, I got to see what Shariq looked like, and I wasn't disappointed at all. He looked to be around six feet, probably a little taller. He had an athletic build that was covered in smooth chocolate skin and tattoos. He had a low haircut that looked like it would be curly if he let it grow longer. His face was outlined with a thick beard that looked soft as hell. I knew it was crazy to lust after a perfect stranger, but here I was doing just that. Surprisingly, his sister kept in touch with me. I had no objections since I really didn't know anyone here and that would give me a reason to keep in touch with her fine ass brother. Like now, she was currently at my house sitting in my chair, letting me do a freehand set on her.

"Has my brother called you back?" she asked.

"No. Not since the first day that we talked," I responded.

"He gets on my nerves because instead of asking me to find out information about you, he could be doing it himself." She blabbed.

"He's been asking about me?" I blushed.

"Like a muthafucka. He asked me how you looked and everything." I caught myself smiling as I thought about the fact that I was crushing over a man I never met. A fuckin' felon, but hell, those were the best kind.

"So, this last-minute nail appointment was to get information out of me?" I quizzed.

"Yes, and no. I wanted to feel you out because I am very protective of my brother," she stated. "I also came because I've been lurking on your business page and saw your fire ass designs and I had to come see for myself. These other hoes out here be tripping and overcharging and still don't do much of shit." I internally popped my collar because I knew I was the shit and soon enough I was going to snatch up my competitor's clients. That's if I already hadn't.

"I appreciate you giving me a try. I want to build my clientele here, even though I have most of my regulars that travel to me. It wouldn't help to add a dozen or two more." I smirked.

"Damn you like that?" she asked.

"Just like that." I boasted.

"Well, okay then." I finished up her set, and we talked about a little bit of everything. I knew that she was older than Shariq by two years at thirty.

They were raised by their mother and, from what she explained, she's a live wire. The total opposite of my own mother. I grew up with my parents in the military. They were both in the Army. My father was deployed to the war in Iraq when I was four. He was only there for three months before he was killed. I didn't quite understand what was going on, but I knew I no longer had a father. My mother dived headfirst into her work, so she was rarely home. I spent a lot of time with Lex and her mother, which was one of the reasons we became so close. Lex and her mother stayed close by the base in the hood and that's where I met my baby daddy, Ramone. He was older by four years at twenty and a street nigga. The ones with the braids and gold teeth and nice car and clothes. I was smitten and thought I was hot shit when he started paying attention to me. That went on until I got pregnant a year later with our son, Kyren. At seventeen, I was a teenage mother who didn't have the support of her mother to guide her. It wasn't until Ramone got locked up the first time that my mother stepped in and started helping with him. We still didn't have the perfect relationship, but we had one and I appreciated it.

We continued to have small talk as I finished up the medium length French tip nails that were all adorned with different colored designs and rhinestones. This was the best part of my job because I always had complete creative control when it came to the designs. I just asked what colors they wanted, and I did my thing. When I was done, Shadai inspected her nails and smiled at me.

"Oh, baby. You just made a new customer. I'll definitely be back," she confirmed.

"I'll be right here."

"Ma, you about done? I'm hungry." Kyren stuck his head inside the door and asked.

"Yes. I'm finishing up, but you can get a snack before it's ready." He nodded and darted back out the room and headed toward the kitchen.

"He's tall. You have him in sports?" she asked.

"No, not yet. We were actually going next week to look at a few options for him to make friends," I stated.

She nodded then said, "hey, I know it may sound crazy, but why don't you come to the hearing tomorrow? I mean, you did help us in a way. You can go and show your support," she said. I thought about it for a minute. It wouldn't hurt and I would be able to see his fine ass in person.

"I don't know, Shadai. I got y'all in contact with one another and that money was enough."

"First of all, call me Shay, and girl, that money wasn't nothing. Come, show your face and then afterwards you can leave." I thought about what she said. It wouldn't cause any harm to go and show some support. Before I could respond, she did.

"No pressure. Court starts at ten. If you make

it, just text me and I'll let you know where to come." She sent me her payment via Apple Pay and got up to leave. When I locked up, I went to clean up my work room and headed for the kitchen to fix me and Kyren dinner. Tonight consisted of baked beans with sausage and white rice. I let Kyren choose, and this was his choice, and after Shay came for an impromptu appointment, I wasn't mad at all.

While I was cutting up the onions, bell peppers and sausage to sauté before adding them to the beans, I called Lex to let her sip all this damn tea I've collected in two days. She answered on the second ring.

"What it is hoe...wassup?" her crazy ass answered.

"Why must you be like this?" I laughed.

"Shit, when I find out, I'll let you know. Wassup though?"

I took a deep pull from my pen before I explained to my best friend what happened over the past two days. By the time I was done, her usually boisterous ass was quiet as a mouse.

"You ain't gonna say nothing?" I asked.

"Girl...I was trying to look this fine ass nigga up. Bitch, if you don't go tomorrow, I will because gah damn." I could only shake my head at this crazy ass girl.

"You think he needs some money on his books? I can get some money from Jarvis and send it." I knew her ass was serious as hell.

"Bitch, you will not take that man's money and spend it on another man."

"Shit, he takes it and spends it on other bitches, so why not?" I could hear her shrug through the phone.

"Besides, I don't know anything about this man. Why would I go to his bond hearing?" I asked.

"Because clearly he wants to thank you face to face if his sister asked you to come." I sat and thought about it, and she was persuading me more and more that I should just go and show my face.

"I'll see how I feel in the morning. Right now, I'm about to finish cooking so I can chill out the rest of the night in front of the TV with my pen. I know that Ky and Alex gonna be on the game all night, so I won't have to worry about him."

It didn't take long to get dinner ready and after we ate, Kyren went back into his room and started yelling at the game again. I went into my room and showered. As soon as I was finished and got into bed with my remote and pen, a Facetime call through on my phone.

"Who the hell is this?" I said out loud.

It kept ringing, and hesitantly I answered. When the call connected, I got the surprise of my life. On the other end of the phone was Shariq, looking fine as hell even in his orange jumpsuit.

"Wassup, shorty?" He asked with a smile.

Stunned, I still couldn't even find the words until he spoke again.

"You gon' say something?" he asked, breaking me out of my trance.

"Uhm...how are you calling me?" I asked.

"I know some people. What you got going on?" He was looking around me like he was searching for something.

"Nothing. I just started my wind down from the day. I didn't do too much. I had an impromptu nail appointment, but I'm gonna assume that you know about that already." I smirked.

"I'on know what you talkin' about, shorty." He lied.

"Janelle," I corrected.

"My bad, Janelle." He flashed a perfect white smile at me. The pictures I saw of him online didn't do this man any justice. In his pictures, he wore a gold and diamond grill. I can only assume it wasn't in now because of his current situation.

"Tell me about your appointment," he said.

"Well, it was your sister." I started, but his gaze never wavered.

"Oh yeah? How'd that go?" he asked.

"It went well. We got to talk and get to know one another. She's nice. She also let me know that she was very protective of her baby brother."

"She stay calling me a fuckin' baby." he interrupted.

"There's nothing wrong with that. I wish I had an older sibling."

"You're the oldest?" he asked.

"I'm the only. My father died in Iraq and my mother never remarried or had any more children," I revealed.

"Damn, shorty. I'm sorry to hear that." I appreciated the sincerity in his voice.

"I got over it. I got wild, but I got over it." I took a pull from my pen and held the smoke in for a little while before I blew it back out.

"You smoke?" he asked. All I did was hold up my pen because he just saw me use it.

"Yeah. I would rather use pens than actual weed. I don't like smelling like smoke."

"I respect it." We were quiet for a while, and he finally started talking again.

"Did Shay ask you to come tomorrow?"

"I thought you didn't know she came?" I smirked, and he returned it.

"I didn't say I didn't know she came. I said I didn't know about an appointment." He flashed that smile that started to make my body tingle.

"Yeah, she told me," I responded.

"And?" he countered.

"And I told her I would think about it," I stated. I saw him look around before turning his attention back to me.

"Aye, I need to go, shorty, but I'll see you tomorrow." He stated with finality.

"Goodnight, Shariq."

"Night, shorty." He hung up the phone and I just say there for a minute before getting out of bed to find something to wear to court in the morning.

What the hell am I doing?

Chapter Five

Shariq

It was finally Monday morning, and I was up early before count so I could be refreshed before court. Since Douglas was working, I had the luxury of showering before anyone else. I didn't want to be around them niggas anyway, but they knew better. After I showered, I thought about calling Janelle, but I decided against it. I would wait to see if she showed up on her own without me calling her. I did call my mama, though. I know she was going to be pissed that I'm just now calling, but I wanted to get through the weekend without worrying her too much. I went back into my cell and retrieved the phone that I had Douglas bring me. When she answered, I knew she was skeptical of who could be calling her this early in the morning, but knowing her, she already knew.

"Shariq, I should kick yo' muthafuckin' ass. Why are you just calling me, boy?" she fussed.

"How did you know it was me?" I asked.

"Who else would be calling me this damn early from a damn number I don't know? Hell, Spam Likely even has the decency to wait until after ten."

I had to laugh at her outburst because Dawn Carter was definitely a piece of work.

"Well, since you know it's me. Are you coming to court with Shay?"

"Yeah, I'll be there. I'm riding with Shay. She should be here any minute now." She confirmed. I felt bad for dragging my mama down to the courthouse yet again. That shit tore me up every time.

"Ma," I called out.

"I know, Shariq. I'll see you later."

"Alright. I love you, Ma."

"I love you too, baby." I hung up the phone with my mama right before Douglas walked up to the entrance of the cell.

"Frost, your lawyer is upfront. She wants to go over a few things before you go down," he said.

Nodding, I got up and followed him out of the cell and down the narrow hallway. When we got to the room, Erielle was already sitting, waiting.

"Wassup, E?" I greeted.

"Hey, Shariq. I just wanted to go over a few things." She started going through her folder, flipping through papers.

"I'm hoping it's some good shit because I don't want to be here after today. I got shit to do and I know they gon' try some fuck shit after the hearing, so I need to get my shit in order." I knew they would

41

more than likely set a high ass bail and I definitely had the money to post it, but I needed to make sure them muthafuckas gave me one first.

"Well, I need them to do that shit because I got shit to do and I can't do it behind these fuckin' walls." I expressed.

"I know Shariq, and I'm going to do my best to get you out of here until they have a hearing. With you being on probation, I'm pretty sure one is going to follow this." I nodded at her and got up to leave. Douglas was still standing outside when we opened the door. After letting me know that she would meet me in the courtroom, she went one way and Douglas took me another. I would usually talk to the nigga, but I was more concerned with getting the fuck out of here.

When we got inside the courtroom, I glanced around until I saw my family sitting in the second row behind the defendant's table. When I noticed my sister, she gave me a smirk and tilted her head to the side. Following her direction, I noticed Janelle was sitting next to her, with a little boy sitting right beside her. I nodded at my family before taking a seat and waiting to get this shit over with. It took about twenty minutes for the judge to come out and when he did; it was an old white man. I knew right then and there I was fucked. After the bailiff had us to stand and waited for the judge to be seated, I watched intently as he looked over the papers in front of him.

"I see we have a Mr. Shariq Carter present with us today. Convicted felon. More than a few drug charges. Assault charges, and currently on probation." I saw him look over his glasses at me and I silently cursed to myself.

"I see the State has requested no bail. Defense, do you have anything to say?" he asked, looking deadpan at Erielle.

"Yes, Your Honor. My client, Mr. Carter, should be granted bail. He hasn't been in any trouble since he's been released and he's a loving father who is the sole provider for his daughter," she stated.

"Who does the child live with?" he asked.

"She lives with her mother, Your Honor."

"Mr. Carter, do you have a support system?" He turned his line of questioning to me.

"I do, Your Honor. My mother, sister, best friend, and uncle stand in and help me," I responded.

"That's good to know, Mr. Carter, because I'm going to deny your bail. You will remain in custody of the Duval county jail until your hearing date. Case dismissed." He banged his gavel and mugged the fuck out of his ass.

"The fuck, E?" I turned toward Erielle.

"I told you this was going to be hard, but I'll be working on it," she stated.

"This is some bullshit. Can you at least get a hearing as soon as possible? I don't want to be in here longer than I have to."

"I'm on it as soon as we leave here," she stated.

"'Preciate it, E." She nodded. I watched as she gathered her things and Douglas approached our table. I beckoned for my family to come over before he took me back.

"Aye, let me holla at my people real quick," I told him, and he nodded. He walked us to a small hallway and my mama was the first to speak.

"Damn it, Shariq. I won't curse you like I want to, but as soon as you get your black ass out, I'm letting you have it for the old and the new," she said before pulling me into a hug.

"I know, Ma," was all I said. Shay approached me next.

"Stay on top of E. I trust her, but I want to make sure she's on top of this shit. Make sure Riah is straight for me, too."

"You don't even have to ask that. I got you and call me later." I hugged my sister and then took my focus to Janelle and the lil' boy I assumed was her son.

"Come here, shorty," I said.

"You're determined not to say my name, huh?" she said with a smirk.

"You'on like when I call you 'shorty'?" She blushed. "Nah, but for real. I appreciate you for coming today. That shit meant a lot to me for real. I know this may be asking a lot, but do you think I can still call and talk to you while I'm here? It'll help me stay sane and for some reason, your lil' husky voice does that for me." I smirked as I watched her tawny skin flush.

"I think I can do that. It's not like I do anything, anyway." She shrugged.

"Bet. You mind if I get a hug before this nigga gotta take me back?" I asked, trying my hand.

She looked at me hesitantly before she walked closer to me and into my embrace. I squeezed her tight and started rubbing my hands down her back.

"Aye, dude. Watch yo' hands," her son said. I couldn't do nothing but smile because he was on the right track.

"My bad, lil' homie. You got it. What's ya name?" I asked.

"Kyren," he stated, poking his lil' chest out.

"Aight, Ky. Make sure you watch out for ya mama until I can come check y'all out. Aight?"

He looked between me and his mama before saying, "I got you." I stuck my fist out and waited until he met it with his smaller one. I told my people goodbye once again before I let Douglas take me back to my cell. I was pissed as a muthafucka, but it wasn't shit I could do about it right now.

Douglas escorted me back to my cell and I've just been sitting in this bitch trying to get my mind right. I knew that bitch ass judge was going to make an example out of me, but I was expecting him to let me go home, only with a high ass bond that he thought I couldn't post. This shit was pissing me off because the more time I sat in the dusty ass place, the more time I had away from my daughter. I tried my best to shake off the unwarranted ill mood that I felt creeping up on me. The only way that I could do that was to call my baby girl and check on her myself. Douglas was still on duty, so I was good to pull out my phone and call my baby girl on FaceTime. She was nosy like her mama, so I knew she would answer.

"Daddy?" she said once our call connected.

"Yeah, baby girl. Wassup? You straight?" I asked, letting my eyes scan over her face for any signs of distress.

"Yes, sir. Auntie Shay called me. How long do you have to be gone this time?" When she asked that, I immediately started feeling like shit.

"I don't know, baby. I'm waiting to talk back to my lawyer, but I'll be here until that happens, and I have to go back to see the judge." I saw the sadness in her eyes, and I swear I was about to break out of this bitch.

"Can I call you on this phone?" she asked innocently.

"Nah, baby girl, but I can call you and I promise to call you every day. Okay?"

"Okay, Daddy." Her little voice cracked, and I had to close my eyes briefly before I tore some shit up. Outside of my mama, I hated disappointing my daughter. I wasn't one of those deadbeat muthafuckas. Even though this may have been out of my control at the moment, I should've been smarter. I watched her pout a little longer before I wasn't able to take that shit anymore.

"Where your mama?" I asked her about her annoying ass mama.

"She's in her room."

"Go take her the phone for me." I watched as she got up and took the phone to Mariah's room. I heard her knock, then Mariah yell from the other end.

"My daddy wants to talk to you," I heard her say. I heard Mariah suck her teeth, but immediately after, her face came into view. Mariah was fine as hell; she was just ratchet as all hell and aggravating as fuck.

"You really love that place, don't you?" she said, making me instantly regret asking to speak to her ass.

"Don't try to get fly with me, MaMa. I just wanted to keep you in the loop of what was going on. I didn't get a bond today and I have to stay here until they give me a hearing. I got my lawyer on top of everything. Shay and Cruz gonna make sure y'all straight until I get out."

47

"I don't need nobody to look out for us," she sassed.

"Don't start yo' shit, Mariah. I know how you like to do and if my mama and sister tell me you on some bullshit, you gon' wish they kept me in this bitch. You got me?" I damn near growled.

"Whatever, Frost." She handed the phone back to my baby girl, and she still had that pitiful look on her face.

"Listen, I want you to be a good girl for me, aight?" She nodded. "I love you, baby girl."

"I love you too, Daddy." I hung that muthafuckin' phone up so fast I thought I cracked the screen. I checked the time and decided to give Cruz a call before they did their shift change. Douglas would be leaving, but he assured me that his partner would look out while he was here.

I dialed Cruz's number and waited for him to answer. He did on the third ring.

"Yo," his voice boomed.

"Damn nigga, you sound happy as hell."

"Frost?" he asked incredulously.

"Who else would it be, nigga?" I snapped.

"My bad, nigga. You straight?" I knew he wasn't trying to be funny, but that shit pissed me off. I didn't act on it though because what good would it do? Instead, I diverted the conversation.

"Did you get my car?" I asked.

"Yeah, I got it."

"Bet. Take my clothes to Boogie."

"Why?" he asked.

"Because I said so. The fuck you mean?"

"Aye, chill. I was just asking. I'll hit that nigga up and take it to him. You need me to do anything else?" he asked.

"Yeah. I need you to make sure Mariah and my baby girl good while I'm in here. I just talked to them, and my baby fucked me up, asking how long I was going to be in here this time."

"Damn, bruh. I got you. I'll swing by there after I go see Boogie. You straight?" he asked again.

"Yeah. I had Shay take care of that.

"Aight. I'll go holla at her too," he acknowledged.

"Bet."

I hung up the phone with Cruz just as they were getting ready to do shift change. I stepped outside of my cell and came face to face with this nigga named Mooney. I couldn't stand that muthafucka and I guess he thought he was safe in this bitch. I mugged that nigga as I prepared to pass him, and I guess he grew some balls and shoulder checked me on his way by. That was a bold fuckin' move and the wrong one. There was no need to ask that nigga anything. I beat his ass right there in the middle of the quad until I felt multiple arms grabbing at me.

"The fuck off me!" I roared.

I looked on as they helped his bitch ass off of the floor and escorted my black ass to the hole. This was already starting off all wrong.

Fuck!

Chapter Six

Janelle

A week later...

I haven't talked to Shariq since the day at his bond hearing. I wanted to be in my feelings, but I didn't have the right to. Or did I? I shook the thought from my head as I cleaned up the mess from my last client. I didn't have any more set for the day and just as I was about to head to Kyren's room to check on him, my phone rang, and it was Shay calling.

"Hey, Shay," I greeted.

"Hey, sis," she countered.

Sis? I thought to myself.

"Don't sound so surprised. What you doing today?" she asked.

"Uhm, I just got finished with my last client of the day. I had nothing else planned. I'll probably find something for me and Ky to do," I responded.

"Well, why don't you and nephew come and go out with me, and we can stop by my mama's house afterwards to eat. Alonzo is out of town, and I'm bored." I didn't miss her calling Kyren her nephew, but that was a bit premature.

"Uhm, I don't know. I haven't heard from Shariq since the hearing and I don't want to overstep boundaries," I stated honestly.

"That's what this is about?" I heard her giggle. "Chy, Frost got his ass locked in the hole for beating a nigga's ass after the hearing. One of the guards was from around the way and told me. I'm pretty sure that won't be the first time, but it better be before he goes back to court."

"Frost?" I repeated.

"Yeah, that's his street name and apparently he had to show the nigga," she said casually. I sat and thought about it. I had nothing else to do, and I needed to get out the house...Kyren too.

"Okay, I'll meet you. Just text me the details."

"Okay. I just left from picking my niece up, and we can meet somewhere." When she said niece, I was shocked. I mean, Shariq wasn't my man, and I had a child too. I should've expected him to have a child. Hell, the way he looked, I'll have his damn baby too.

"Uhm," I started.

"Come on, Nellie. It's not like you doing anything else," she stated, making me roll her eyes.

"You tried it, but you're right." I laughed.

"Good. I'll send you the location as soon as I find out where this little girl wants to go. We can't make it a spa day because you have a son, but I'll text you back in a few," she confirmed.

"That's fine. Let me go get this boy off of this game and get dressed. We'll meet you later." We hung up, and I got off the couch and headed to Kyren's room. Of course, he was in the middle of a game with Alex.

"Dooda, how long you got on your game?" I asked as I walked in.

"Maybe about thirty minutes. Wassup?" he asked like he was grown.

"Wassup? Boy, you ain't grown." I gave him a stern look. "When you're done, we're going to go hang out with my friend Shay and her niece," I informed.

"Shay? The pretty lady from the courthouse?" he asked with a smirk.

"Yeah, her." I shook my head at him.

"That dude your boyfriend?" he asked. He didn't say anything about Shariq. His mama and sister made us feel welcome and even invited us to lunch, but I declined. I didn't want to give these people the wrong idea, yet here I am getting ready to hang out with his sister and daughter.

"No, he's just a friend," I stated. He gave me an unsure look and went back to his game.

Leaving him in his room, I went back down the hallway to go inside of my room to find something to wear. It was already after five, so I knew the weather would be getting a little cooler later and I didn't know where we were going yet, so I needed to take that into consideration as well. I looked inside of my closet and looked for an outfit. I had a few designer pieces, but I was a SHEIN girl. Their clothes were cute, cheap, and comfortable. I decided on a two-piece cropped tank top and matching leggings with the long duster jacket to match. After getting dressed, I went back into my bathroom and styled my hair. I loved my short hair. I was so easy to upkeep, and I was still cute. After making sure every piece of hair was in place, I grabbed my phone and saw that Shay had texted me with the location. When I looked it up, I saw that it was an indoor go-cart facility. I know Kyren would love that. I went to check on him and he was tying his locs up in a bun. Even though his sides and back were cut, his locs extended to his shoulders.

"You ready?" I asked as he finished with his hair.

"Yes, ma'am." He grabbed his phone off of the dresser and we headed out of the door.

"Ma, where are we going?"

I looked at him through the rearview mirror before I responded.

"Well, Shay invited us to come ride go-carts with her and her niece," I let him know.

"Her niece?" He frowned. "She doesn't know any boys?"

Laughing, I responded, "I don't know, Ky. All I know is that she has a niece. We can find out about a nephew, though." He still didn't look too happy about playing with a girl, but he would get over it.

We rode the thirty-minute drive in silence minus the radio playing my favorite playlist. I rapped along with Glorilla and Megan Thee Stallion as they talked about these wanna be niggas. I pulled up to the venue in record time and me and Kyren went inside in search of Shay and her niece. We found them in line waiting to pay, so we walked up to them. Shay saw us approaching and greeted us.

"Hey! Y'all made it." She smiled.

"Yeah, traffic wasn't that bad coming from the Southside."

"That's a good thing." She looked toward her niece, and you would think it was her daughter because they looked like twins. They both had smooth caramel skin and bright brown eyes that resembled Shariq's. The little girl had her hair in a big, bushy, curly ponytail with her little edges smoothed to perfection.

"This is my niece, Shariah. Shariq's daughter." She introduced us, and Shariah gave us a small smile. I saw the look on Kyren's face, and it looked as if he was changing his mind about playing with girls.

"Hi, Shariah. I'm Janelle and this is my son, Kyren." I introduced us.

"You're pretty," she complimented.

"And so are you." We got the kids their tickets and found a table not far from the obstacle course. We got settled and watched them before Shay started talking.

"You know, Riah asked me if you were her daddy's girlfriend?"

"Kyren asked me the same thing." We shared a laugh, but she quickly got serious.

"You know Riq doesn't let women who aren't her mother get close to her," she informed.

"That's good to know because we're just friends...if I can call it that."

"Keep telling yourself that. I know my brother. At first he was showing his gratitude for getting in touch with me for him. Then it was your voice." She smirked. "That fool literally sat on the phone and said, 'I don't know what it is about her lil' husky ass voice, but I can't shake it.' Now you tell me if that's just friends. Hell, he paid for my nails. Why do you think you had such a hefty tip? This outing is all on him too," she stated.

"I thought you said he was on lockdown?" I found myself asking. The knowing smirk on her face didn't go unnoticed, but I ignored her ass.

"I thought you didn't care?" she smirked. "Anything dealing with Shariah he funds, whether it's with me or her raggedy ass mama. Why did you think I insisted on paying for Kyren? He would've done the same thing." I sat and listened to her tell me about her brother, and I couldn't help but be intrigued. I didn't know if it was because I hadn't been with a man in months or I was genuinely interested in him. Hell, he was in jail. What kind of relationship could we possibly have?

"I see the wheels turning in your head. Let me give you a piece of advice. Listen to your heart and not your head. My brother may not be in the best predicament right now, but he's a good man, and I'll put that on Savannah and her meddling ass mama. I'm not just saying this because he's my brother, either. This isn't his first rodeo, but this time it's different. I saw the way he looked at you when you were at court. My brother likes you and when he feels the way, I'm pretty sure he's feeling about you. Nothing will stop him from getting what he wants. All I ask is that you don't hold his current situation against him." I listened to Shay as she talked so highly of her brother, and I must say that she did one hell of a job. I wouldn't say that I would jump headfirst into a relationship, but I will continue to talk to him as long as he wanted to.

As we sat and talked, we watched as the kids ran through every obstacle course there. When they came running over to us, letting us know that they were hungry, we decided it was time to go.

"Ma, where we going to eat?" Kyren asked.

"My nana can cook us something," Shariah mentioned.

"Ooh, nanas know how to cook good. Ma, can we go?" he asked. His statement made me and Shay laugh.

"I don't know, Ky." I started.

"Yeah, nephew. Y'all can come." She looked at me and said, "just follow me." Instead of arguing or refusing to go, Kyren and I headed toward our car, but not without asking if Shariah could ride with us. I was hesitant because I didn't know these people well enough to be responsible for their kid, yet here I was loading them up inside the back of my matte green Infinite QX55. I saw Shay pull out in front of us and I prayed the whole time I had this little girl inside of my vehicle.

I remembered her saying that their mother lived on the Southside of town and surprisingly I didn't stay far from the area. Maybe fifteen or twenty minutes, depending on traffic. We pulled up to a nice house that had a well-manicured lawn and driveway that led to a garage. I parked behind Shay and the children got out before I even stopped good.

"Come on, Ky. Let's go see what my nana has in here to eat." Shariah practically dragged Kyren into the house behind her. Shay met me at my car and nudged me.

"Girl, come on here. My mama ain't gon' do nothing to you. I will let you know that she can read people very well and if she feels as if you have an ill or nasty spirit, she'll let it be known. Other than that, you're good and I think that you'll be perfectly fine." Her words didn't help me at all, but I followed her inside of the house, anyway. When we walked in, I took immediate notice that everything was decorated in different hues of brown with gold accents. It smelled like lemons throughout, but I also smelled something frying. When we came into view, she already had the kids sitting at the counter with fruit cups.

"'Bout time y'all got in here. These babies are starving," she said. I looked at Kyren like he'd lost his mind.

"Kyren Michai. I know you're not acting like I don't feed you," I scolded. Before he could respond, Shariq and Shadai's mother interrupted him.

"Leave that baby alone. My grandbaby came inside and said that she was hungry, and I wasn't about to let this baby be hungry. Anyway, it's nice seeing you again, Janelle. How you been, baby?" I was almost shocked at the way she put me in my place, then wanted to know how I was doing, but I remember Shadai saying that this was how she was.

"It's nice seeing you again," I replied.

"Did Shay tell you what happened with that nappy headed ass boy of mine?" she asked. I looked between her and the kids before responding. They were engrossed in whatever they were watching on their iPads.

"Yes ma'am, she did."

"I hope you don't hold it against him. He brought his current situation on his self, but he does try to stay low and out the way, but we know how that can go sometimes," she explained. I was really baffled at the way they were advocating for this man, and I was sitting my ass right here and believing everything they were saying.

"I'm not saying he's a bad person. I just haven't had the opportunity to talk to him any further to get to know him," I stated honestly.

"All that's going to change. Now you and Shay come on here and help me fix this food. My grandbabies hungry." I was thrown off by her calling Kyren her grandbaby, but I didn't want to start anything, so I just went along with it. She was almost done anyway before we came, so all me and Shay had to do was set the table. It felt good doing stuff like this because I rarely got a chance to do stuff like this with my own mother.

As we ate, we held small talk, and they got to know a little more about me and Kyren. They seemed to be genuine about the things they were saying, and I appreciated it. Once we were done, Shay and I helped her clean the kitchen while the kids went to play. We heard the doorbell ring and Ms. Dawn went to open it. A few seconds later, we heard a loud, ratchet sounding voice flow through the house.

"Mariah, don't bring your ass in here with all that loud ass talking. You know I'll put yo' ass right back on the other side of the door," she said.

"Where's my baby?" I heard her ask. They finally came into view and when she noticed me, she turned up her nose. She was a very pretty girl, but I could tell she was one of those. Meaning, one who felt threatened by any other woman regardless of who they were. We stood around the same height. Her skin was the color of milk chocolate, and her hair was slayed to the gawds with the thirty-inch bust down that she wore. Designer covered her thick body that I'm sure she paid for, but it was still banging, nonetheless. Moments later, I heard the kids come back into the living room, where Shariah went straight to her mother with Kyren in tow.

"Hey, Ma. This is my new friend Kyren. His mom is daddy's friend." When she said that, I could've sworn that I saw Mariah get two shades darker.

"I know y'all ain't got my baby 'round no random ass bitch," she snapped. See, that was her first, second, and third strike. I may have been a pretty bitch, but I was also a crazy one and she was about to find out the fast way.

"Aye, listen. I don't know you and you don't know me. I don't know how you usually address other people, but you don't have any more times to call me out of my name. Now, out of respect for Ms. Dawn and these children, I won't drag yo' ass, but don't test me. This was your one and only chance to get buck with me. Don't let this pretty face and these nails fool you. I'll slaughter yo' ass. Kyren let's go." I was pissed off. Not only did this bitch call me out of my name, but I had to show my ass in front of people and my son, but I didn't play about my respect.

As I was gathering our things, Mariah stood there seething mad like I gave a fuck. Shay volunteered to walk us out, and I heard Ms. Dawn cursing her ass out for disrespecting her house. Once I was in my car, Shay looked at me and smirked.

"What?" I asked.

"Welcome to the family," was all she said. I opted not to ask her to elaborate. I waited for Kyren to get situated in the back before I pulled off. As I drove home, I thought about if I really wanted to do this. I didn't even know this man, but his family was already accepting me and my son. My mind was all over the place, but I wasn't about to let it get the best of me. I would go home and smoke my pen and let my mind settle. Whatever I had to do, my pen would always settle my thoughts.

Chapter Seven

Shariq

They finally let me out of that damn hole after ten fuckin' days. When Douglas escorted me back to my cell, he told me that they moved Mooney's bitch ass to another quad. That was their best bet because I would've beaten that nigga's ass every time that I saw his ass. Because he wanted to be a brave bitch, he kept me away from my daughter and my damn girl. Yeah, I may have just met Janelle, but I swear when I hugged her, our hearts instantly bonded. I was always a nigga that knew what he wanted, and I wanted Janelle. Once I made it back to my cell, I waited a few minutes before I got pulled out my phone and called my baby girl. I would hit everyone else up after her. She would always be my top priority and I wanted her to always know that. I dialed her number via FaceTime and waited for her to pick up, but she never did. I tried two more times and still got the same thing. Instead of thinking the worst, I called my baby mama. When I dialed her number, I got the same results from when I called Shariah. That pissed me off because that meant Mariah was up to her bullshit ass games. After not getting an answer from my daughter and her ignorant ass mama, I called my sister. When the call connected and she saw the look on my face, she knew immediately what was wrong.

"What happened?" I asked, knowing something had to go down.

"Mariah came to Ma's while Janelle and Kyren were there. Riah introduced her as your friend, and Mariah flipped." My baby mama didn't like it when I entertained anyone but for someone to be at my mama's house, she knew I had to be feeling them something serious.

"Fuck!" I grumbled.

"Oh, but trust, my new sis got her together real quick." I saw the smirk on her face and knew my baby handled business. I knew she didn't play that disrespectful shit when she kept correcting me on her name.

"That's good to know, but damn, I ain't even got the girl to agree to be my damn woman yet, and she's already fucking the shit up for me." I huffed.

"I don't think she did too much damage because we went out to dinner again last night. Alonzo just got back into town today, so I told her I would catch up with her later." I liked the fact that they were hanging out and getting to know each other. That meant everything to me because if my mama or sister didn't like you, then it wasn't too much I could do with you but fuck you and send you on your way.

"I still need to do damage control, though." I was already thinking of ways to apologize to Janelle for Mariah's bullshit.

"I see the look on your face. Go call your girl." Shay smirked.

"Yeah, I need to do that. Go check on my baby for me and tell Mariah to stop fuckin' playing wit' me." I knew by me telling her that she would probably go tighten Mariah's ass up and I that's just what I wanted.

"Oh, and if it helps. She's not mad at you, but she doesn't want to get caught up in Mariah's bullshit," she informed. I appreciated her looking out for me, but I got this. I wasn't going to tell her that shit, though.

"I 'preciate that, sis. Let me call and see how much damage control I gotta do."

"Alright. Try to call me later. Love you, fathead."

"Love yo' big ass head, too." I hung up the phone with my sister and immediately called Janelle's number. The call went straight to the voicemail, and I knew her ass didn't have me blocked too. To make sure, I called her again, only for her to pick up this time. When I saw her pretty ass popped up on the screen, I couldn't help but take her bare face in. Her skin had a natural glow to it that let you know that she stayed up on her skincare. Her short hair wasn't curled like it was the last time I saw her, but she still looked beautiful to me. She still hadn't said anything, so I decided to speak up.

"Wassup, shorty?" I spoke.

"Hey, Shariq," she countered. I could tell that she was in her feelings, so I wasn't about to prolong the inevitable.

"Look, I heard about the shit that Mariah did, and I want to apologize for that shit. Her ass is always doing the most all the damn time."

"It's okay. You don't have to apologize for her."

"But I do. How can I convince you to stay my girl and she's already starting her bullshit?" I noticed her eyes bucked when I said that.

"Your girl? Shariq, I never agreed to be your girl. You didn't even ask me." I can tell her own words surprised her because she started stammering over her words.

"I-I didn't mean to say that. I...uhm." I cut her off.

"You want me to ask you to be my girl?" I asked, staring into her sexy brown eyes, almost boring into her soul.

"I...that's not what I said."

"But what if that's what I want to do? What if I want you to be my girl?" I was waiting for her to respond, but she never did.

"Look, I know you probably think that I'm bullshittin' you, but I'ma call my sister and she's going to get you straight. After talking to her, you'll know how serious I am. How about that?" I waited for her to start speaking again, and it felt like forever, but when I heard that sexy ass voice of hers again, my heart stalled.

"You know Kyren asked were you my boyfriend," she revealed.

"Oh yeah? What you tell my lil' homie?"

"I told him the truth. That we were just friends."

"Friends? Yeah, I need you to go ahead and let him know that friend shit is dead. As a matter of fact, where is he now?" I stared at her and waited for her to answer.

"He's in his room on that damn game. I swear I can't wait to get him in some sort of activities so he can find something to do besides play that game with my godson all day."

"I'll make a few calls and get some shit into motion for him. He needs to get outside and enjoy some fresh air. Hell, I even had Riah playing AU basketball. My baby's a beast with her jump shot, too." I beamed at the thought of my baby girl.

"You know she asked was I your girlfriend, too?"

"I know you tried that friend shit, but I'll straighten her out, too. Can't have her thinking we're just friends just in case her and Ky plotting some shit. Gotta let 'em know they're going to be siblings." I flashed her my signature smile. I could've sworn I saw her melt. If I didn't think she would curse me out, I'd ask her to let me see something.

"You got any clients today?" I asked. She got up to walk away from the phone and her fat ass in those tiny ass pink shorts came into view. I could barely concentrate when I saw her in nothing but that small ass gray tank top on and I could tell she didn't have on a bra. When she came back, she had another phone in her hand.

"You got a trap phone, or that's for your hoes?" I found myself asking. She looked up at me and smirked.

"Sounds like you're a lil' jealous."

"Not hardly. I just needed to see who needed to be eliminated. You might as well gon' and tell them niggas to fall the fuck back because I'on share, shorty. As a matter of fact, let them know that Frost is yo' nigga. They'll get the picture." She just stared at me blankly but didn't respond right away.

"You heard me, shorty?"

"I heard you, but are you done?" Shorty had a fly ass mouth, and I couldn't wait to tame that. "If you are, then I can let you know that this is my work phone. What I need with a trap phone or a hoe phone? Do I look like I need either?" she quizzed.

"My bad, baby. I didn't mean to get you upset. We can't have our first argument, and I'm not there to fix it." I made sure to drop my voice a few octaves so she could hear the desire in it. I watched as she blinked a few times before swallowing.

"Uhm, I only have a client that's coming from Savannah. She won't come until after work, so I'm free until then," she informed me.

"Savannah, huh? They really coming to see you like that, shorty?"

"And is." She smirked.

"I like that shit, shorty. A fuckin' go-getter." She blushed. I got distracted when I saw Douglas standing at the door of my cell. I was so caught up in Janelle that I didn't even hear the nigga. I'm glad he's on duty and not nobody else.

"Aye, Frost. Your lawyer is here," he mentioned. I nodded and put my finger up to signal for him to give me a minute.

"Aye, baby. I need to go see what my lawyer wants. Hopefully, she has some good news for me."

"Okay." she sounded like she was disappointed, and I hated that shit already.

"Hey, don't look like that. How about I set it up for you to come see me tomorrow?" I saw her eyes light up for a quick second before she squinted.

"Can you do that? Don't I have to wait for your specific days" she asked.

"You'll learn, baby. I'll call you later, aight?"

"Okay." I hung up the phone and already felt like shit.

"E, you better have some good news to tell me," I said before putting my phone up and following Douglas to the visitation room.

When I got there, E was already sitting at the desk and from the look on her face, I already knew that she was about to say some shit that I didn't want to hear. I pulled out the chair that was opposite of hers and sat down facing her.

"By the look on your face, I know you're about to say some shit that I don't like." I wasn't about to sit here and let her fiddle around. I needed to know what I was up against.

"Well, Shariq. It's like this. If you have a hearing, they can sentence you to ten years with a minimum of five, and that's just for the gun." I looked at her like she had lost her mind, even though she wasn't the one coming up with this bullshit.

"And what's the option if I don't go back to court?"

"They're offering to let you finish the rest of your probation in jail. Once you complete your sentence, your probation will be over and done with." This was the better option, but I didn't want to spend the next six months in this bitch, especially if I wanted to start a relationship with Janelle. *Would she wait six months? Would she hold a nigga down?* I had so many fuckin' thoughts running through my head that I couldn't even fuckin' think straight. Then, on top of that, I would be missing out on my baby girl. School would be back in before I got out and I would miss that shit. I knew my mama and Shay would step in during my absence, but I hated that they had to even do that. Six months was better than ten years, but I hated to give these muthafuckas anymore of my time. But I didn't have a choice.

"They gave you the paperwork?" I asked. I know they didn't send her here without it.

"They did." She opened her briefcase and pulled out a folder and handed it to me. I read over everything before taking the pen that she offered me and signed my name and my life over for the next six months. After I slid the paper and pen back over to her, I slid down in the chair and folded my arms across my chest.

"So now what?" I asked.

"Now, your property of Duval County for the next six months," she stated solemnly. I watched as she collected her things and exited the room. I didn't get up right away because I was trying to wrap my head around the fact that I was going to be here for the next six months and away from my family and my new girlfriend.

Fuck, this was about to be a long ass six months.

Chapter Eight

Janelle

Today was supposed to be the day that I was set to visit Shariq. I couldn't go on the original day that he had planned because something went down, and they locked the jail down. He had it set up for me to come in as his new lawyer. I didn't know shit about being a lawyer, but here I was in my room looking over my reflection in the mirror admiring the sleeveless black and white color block dress that stopped right above my knees and a matching pair of pumps. I had a designer laptop bag that I used as my briefcase so that my look would be complete. Shay volunteered to let Kyren stay the night with her and Alonzo. I was apprehensive at first but I after she convinced me everything would be okay; I let him stay. He was excited to have another auntie and an uncle that he was ready to go. After being satisfied with my appearance, I grabbed my things and was out the door.

It took me twenty-five minutes to get downtown. I hated coming down here because traffic was always crazy with all these one-way streets. I pulled into the jail's parking lot and found a parking spot not far from the front. When I went inside, I told them my name and my purpose of being here. These people really didn't give a fuck because they didn't ask for any proof of anything. Just let me back and escorted me into a room with white walls and a small table with three chairs in the middle. I took a seat at the table, fumbling with my hands as I waited for Shariq to grace me with his presence.

"What the hell are you doing, Janelle?" I asked myself. No sooner than the words left my mouth, he was swaggering inside of the room, looking like chocolate-covered sin. That orange uniform didn't do his body any justice. The shirt was opened and revealed a white tank top underneath that clung to his tattooed covered chest. His pants weren't hanging ridiculously off of his ass, but they fit perfectly, giving off the perfect silhouette of his print. I didn't break out of my gaze until he was in front of me and pulling me up out of the chair and into his embrace.

"Damn, baby. You look good." He eyed me lasciviously as he spoke. "You smell good, too." He pulled my body into his and put his face into my neck as he let his hands roam freely over my body. I should've felt uncomfortable or out of place, but I didn't. This felt right.

"Th-thank you," I stumbled over my words. He let me go, and I sat back in the chair, and he sat in the one beside me. Never taking his eyes off of me.

"So, what's been going on? Did you talk to my uncle?" he asked. When I mentioned getting Kyren involved in sports, he told me that his uncle was an AU football coach. He called me and said that he had a spot on his team for Kyren if he wanted it. My baby was so excited and so was I.

"Yes, I did. He had a spot on the team for Ky. We went and got his physical already and now just waiting for him to start practice."

"That's wassup, baby. I'll have Ray come by and pick him up for practice. You don't need to be out there with all those niggas, making them think that they have a chance to get wit' yo' fine ass." He smirked, but I saw the desire in his eyes.

"You do know that've I've been a single mother for a while now, so I know how to take my son to sporting events?"

"Yeah, but you're not single, though. It's a difference, baby." He gave me a look that let me know if I wanted to protest it, I shouldn't.

"How many clients you have today?" he asked.

"Six. My first one is at two." I saw him look down at the watch on his wrist before pulling me out the chair.

"Good. That gives us just enough time." By now he had me in his lap, straddling him, and he took over possession of my mouth with his.

"Mmm...wa-wait. We can't do this here." I protested.

"It's cool, baby. My boy is on duty and he's outside of the door. These rooms are soundproof for privacy." As he spoke, he stared me straight into my eyes, grinding my pussy onto his hard dick. This wasn't helping my argument at all.

"Can he see us?" I asked.

"He knows better." As he talked, he reached down into his pants and pulled out his hard dick. My eyes bucked and my mouth watered at the sight of the thick muscle outlined with even thicker veins and a slight curve that made it point toward him. My eyes shot back to him, and he was already staring at me.

"Come on and let's make this shit official."

No other words were needed as he lifted me slightly and pulled my underwear to the side as I positioned myself over him and slid down. The initial impact had me biting down on my bottom lip and clamping my eyes shut.

"Damn, baby. The fuck you doing so tight?" he groaned. "I damn sure ain't complaining but shit. This might not last long." He started moving his hands to my ass, motioning for me to start moving because I was stuck trying to adjust to his size. "Get this dick, mama," he whispered right before taking my bottom lip into his mouth and sucking on it.

I finally found a steady rhythm and started bouncing and grinding on Shariq. This had every right to be locked up behind bars because it should be a crime to be this fuckin' good.

Slap!

"Damn right. Get this shit," he coached, hyping me up.

"Ughn," I moaned out as I ground against him.

I rubbed my hands over his solid chest as I rode him feverishly into my own orgasm.

"B-baby, I'm...shit. I'm about to cum," I whined. When I said that, Shariq grabbed the front of my throat and started fucking me hard and fast from beneath me. I was glad he said this room was soundproof because if not, everybody would've known how he was working me and my pussy over.

"Riq!" I yelped through my orgasm.

"Uhm...hmm. Let that shit go, mama." My damn body was already under his spell because it obeyed his command and I let my juices soak the both of us. I let my head rest on his chest as I tried to catch my breath.

"You good?" he asked. I couldn't verbally respond yet, so I simply nodded.

"Good, now get up and bend over this table." The sound of his deep, husky voice had me ready to move my shit into his cell with him. I knew I couldn't do that, so I simply followed his instructions. I waited with anticipation for him to enter me again, but I was surprised when I was met with his tongue instead.

"Ooh," I cooed in pleasure. I tried to scratch the wood off of this table as he feasted on my kitty. I felt another orgasm start to brew and before it could overcome, he replaced his tongue with his dick in one swift motion.

"Ahh!"

"Gah damn, girl," we moaned out simultaneously.

I held onto the table for dear life as he pumped into me with so much aggression I just knew I would have to be carried out of here. I felt him reach up and run his fingers through the little bit of hair I did have, before dragging it back down and grabbing hold of the back of my neck. His strokes became more powerful and another orgasm shit through me so quick, I didn't even realize it.

"Fuck, baby. I'm finna nut," he called out right before he grunted and succumbed to his own powerful orgasm. It was so powerful that he had my body pressed flat against the table until his dick stopped pulsating inside of me. Slowly, he pulled out and fell back into the chair, pulling me with him.

"Damn, baby. I'on know how I'm going to let you leave after that." He kissed my neck and ran his hands up the front of my body.

"I don't know how I'm going to walk out of here after that," I confessed.

"You need me to get Douglas to walk you out?"

"No, baby. I can walk out by myself. It'll just be

a lil' shameful." I admitted.

"You'll be alright, but check it. We got a few more minutes so handle this for me before you go."

He smirked and glanced back down at his dick, that was now hard again. I gave it a quick thought and turned around and slid back down on him. Both of us moaned out at the feeling and I rode the hell out of my man's dick until I was draining it again.

"Shit, after that, I need a nap. I'll call you later if I can. Douglas shift ends at seven, and I don't know who's coming in yet, but I'll make it happen, aight?" He pulled me into him and squeezed my butt before kissing my neck, then my lips.

"Okay. I need to hurry and get home so I can shower and set up before my client arrives." It was already almost one, so I had to hurry up.

"I'on want to let you go, but I don't want nobody to come down here getting in my business either. Text me and let me know you made it home safely." He gave me one last kiss before tapping on the door. Moments later, the door came open and the officer that escorted me down here appeared.

"Aye, walk her out first, then come back at me," he instructed. The officer simply nodded and walked me out. As soon as I got in my car, I missed his ass already.

This was going to be a long six months.

I made it home in record time to shower and

set up before my appointments. I texted Shariq and let him know that I made it home and he simply replied, 'aight bae'. I smirked at the sentiment and hurriedly got my day started. I was glad that my appointments were all on time. In the middle of my third one, Mone called.

"Hey," I answered.

"Wassup, you busy?" he asked.

"A little. I'm in the middle of a client."

"Well, I won't hold you. I was calling to let you know that I'm coming down this weekend to see Ky. I called, and he told me he was with his new auntie." I knew he was going to try to question me, but he knew we didn't do that.

"That's my business, Mone. Not yours."

"I know, and I'm not trying to get into all that. I trust you wouldn't have our son around anybody. I just wanted to spend some time with him." I couldn't deny that he was a good father. His ass just stayed in and out of jail. Hell, I guess I had a damn type. I shook my head at the thought and told Mone that we would see him on Friday.

I was finally done with my appointments for the day and now I was looking for some food and my pen. Instead of cooking, I decided to order something from Door Dash. While I waited, I called Alexis to fill her in on my day.

"I was just about to call you. How did your visit go with prison bae?" she asked as soon as the call connected.

"Biiitch." I stressed.

"What, bitch. Damn." Lex was impatient as fuck, and I loved fuckin' with her about it.

"Well, the visitation went good, but the dick was even better," I blabbed.

"Hoe, you didn't?" She sounded surprised, but I could hear the smile in her voice.

"I did...twice."

"Well, damn bitch. Hold yo' nigga down then. How was it?" she asked with her nosy ass.

"It was incredible. I can't wait to get that shit when he gets out. If he did my body like that on lockdown, I could only imagine what he'll do once he touches down." I was already having flashbacks of our rendezvous and was anxiously waiting for the next.

"Okay then, bitch. I love that for you. At least one of us finally getting some dick because I refuse to let Jarvis fuck on me. He can go fuck his self for all I care." I burst out laughing at her random outburst. Jarvis must've really fucked up badly this time.

"I mean, I can come back, and we can jump that nigga and his new hoe."

"Girl, fuck them. Nobody is thinking about his free-for-all dick. As long as he still does what he's supposed to do for Alex, then I'm fine." I shook my head in agreement because I had just taken a pull from my pen.

"Girl, guess what?"

"Just tell me." I shook my head.

"Mone called and said that he was coming down this weekend to see Ky."

"Did you tell Shariq?" she asked.

"I just found out. He's supposed to call me back tonight. You think I should tell him? He knows I have a child, so naturally he would have a father."

"Yeah, but you don't want him to think you're being sneaky about some shit."

"We may be new, but he should know better. I shouldn't have to run by him every time Mone wants to see his son. I'm pretty sure he wouldn't tell me every time he goes to his baby mama's house to see or get his daughter." I knew where she was coming from, but the few times I did date, I didn't let them interfere with my co-parenting with Mone. We did what worked for us.

"Okay, boo. I was just trying to help. Let me get in here and get this boy from my mama. I'll call you back later." I hung up with her and went to the door to get my food. After eating, I took my shower and got straight in the bed. Sleep found me before I realized it.

***

The weekend came, and Mone was true to his word and came at Kyren. I let him stay at the hotel with him so they could do their own thing without me in the middle. I got through my appointments and now I was just chilling, watching TV. That didn't last long because Mone was calling me.

"Hello?" I answered.

"You done for the day?" he asked.

"Yep. Y'all having fun?"

"Yeah. You know his greedy ass ready to eat." We both laughed because one thing Kyren did was eat.

"Yeah, that sounds about right."

"You wanna come with us?" he asked.

"I don't think that would be a good idea. This is supposed to be about you and Ky."

"Come on, Nellie. It's just food. I know you're ready to eat too, especially if you hit that pen already." He laughed.

"Don't act like you know me, but where y'all at?" I was already getting up to go inside of the room to find something to wear.

"He asked for The Cheesecake Factory."

"Okay. Give me about thirty minutes, and I'll be there."

"Bet." I hung up the phone with Mone and headed back into the bathroom to freshen up. It didn't take me long to find something to put on. Once again, it was a SHEIN original. This time, it was a burgundy oversized cotton dress that had the image of a black woman on it. I paired it with a pair of Gucci slides. Grabbing my matching Gucci crossbody and shades, I headed out the door and made my way to the restaurant. When I got there, I called, and he directed me to where he and Ky were.

"Damn, you look good, ma," he complimented, with a hug.

"Thank you. Ky, you having fun with your daddy?"

"Yes ma'am. I got the other Jordans I wanted, so you can tell Riq not to worry about it now," he stated. Mone looked at me with his brow raised and I cocked my head to the side, waiting for him to say something. He threw his hands up in mock surrender.

We enjoyed dinner and after Mone paid; we got ready to leave. He was nice enough to walk me to my car. As he stood beside me, I noticed Shariq's best friend and his baby mama walking out, looking a little cozy. They both locked eyes with me but didn't say anything. I guess they expected me to tell Shariq, but that was their business.

"Get home safe. I'll bring him home before I leave tomorrow." I nodded and headed straight home. I pulled my phone out and noticed that Shariq had called me three times. My phone was on vibrate and I didn't hear it. I knew I couldn't text him back, so I sent a text.

Me: Baby, I'm sorry I missed your call. I was

at dinner. I'm headed home now, and you can call me back. I miss you.

I put my phone in the cupholder and made my way home. When I got there, I stripped out of my clothes and tied my hair down and got into bed to wait for my man to call.

Chapter Nine

Shariq

I woke up and saw that Janelle had texted me back after missing my phone calls. I called her back, but I guess she was asleep. I was going to give her time to get up and get ready before I called her back. I went to handle my hygiene and when I was done; I went right for my phone, but the officer approached my cell before I could. Douglas was off today, and his partner didn't come in until tonight.

"Carter, you have a visitor," she stated. My eyebrow rose in confusion, but then I thought it could be Janelle. My mama and sister knew not to come down here.

"Aight." I grabbed my shirt and threw it on and followed her to the visitation area. We went to the main visitation area and when we got to there, I saw Mariah sitting behind the glass with a smug look on his face. I sat down and picked up the phone and started talking.

"Where's Riah?" I asked about my daughter.

"She's with my sister," she stated, rolling her eyes.

"Why hasn't she been to my mama's?" I asked.

"Because I didn't want her around your lil' girlfriend, but I don't think that would be a problem anymore." She had a smirk on her face when she said that.

"The fuck you talkin' about? My girl ain't going nowhere, so you can cut that bullshit." She was starting to piss me off.

"Does she know that?"

"I'm not about to talk about this shit with you." I got ready to hang up the phone until she starting speaking again.

"I saw her last night, and she looked real cute and cozy with some other nigga at The Cheesecake Factory," she causally stated. I didn't even justify what she said. I simply got up and left her ass right there.

When I got back to my cell, I grabbed my phone to call Janelle's ass. She answered on the second ring.

"Hey, ba-" I cut her ass off.

"So, you going on dates and shit now?" I damn near growled.

"What?" she asked, like I was speaking in a language she didn't understand.

"You heard what the fuck I said. That's what you're on?" She excused herself from her client and walked into her room.

"Let me guess. Your triflin' ass baby mama told you that?" She peered at me like she wanted to jump into the phone and beat my ass.

"Oh, so you're not denying it?" I scoffed.

"Shariq, if you let me explain, I can tell you what happened." She pleaded.

"You can't tell me shit. I'm not about to do this shit with you. Ain't no way I can do my time in peace without worrying about if you're fuckin' on the next nigga. I'm good on you." That shit hurt my fuckin' chest, but I wasn't about to let her play with me like this. I looked at her and saw the tears in her eyes, but she was still mugging me.

"Fuck you, Shariq," she snapped as she hung up the phone.

"Fuck!" I bellowed, not caring if one of the guards came or not. I just lost my girl and still had to be in this muthafucka. I didn't give a fuck about nothing at the moment.

Once I calmed down, I called Cruz to check on shit. My personal life was shit, so I hope he was doing what needed to be done on the business side. He answered on the third ring and the nigga sounded like he was whispering.

"The fuck you whispering for?" I asked.

"I was chillin' wit' this shorty. I put her ass to sleep and didn't want to wake her. You know how that goes." He laughed. "Wassup, though?"

"Ain't shit. Just calling to make sure everything is straight. How shit looking?" I asked.

"Everything straight, but why you sound like that? You good?" Cruz and I have been boys for a while, so he knew when some shit was off with me.

"Yeah, I'm straight. I had to let Janelle's ass go, though. She couldn't even hold a nigga down an entire month before she hopped on the next nigga's dick." I vented.

"What you mean the next nigga? You bust shorty down already?" he asked.

"Hell yeah. I had Doug set the shit up. Mariah brought her ass up here this morning without my baby girl just to tell me she saw Janelle out last night with some nigga. She had the nerve to be smiling about the shit too, like she was doing something. I dismissed her ass and called Janelle and dismissed her, too."

"Damn. Did you ask Janelle about it? What did she say?"

"I didn't give her ass time to say shit. The fuck can she say? Mariah always on some dumb shit but I don't think she would lie about some shit like that. She was too eager to throw the shit in my face." I think that's what pissed me off more. My baby mama in my business.

"You need me to go and check the shit out?" he asked.

"Nah. Let her do whatever the fuck she wants

to do. I'm cool off her." I meant that shit. I knew how that shit goes. They say they will hold you down, but as soon as visitation was over and the call ended, you were out of sight, out of mind.

"Aight. Holla at me if you need me to do anything, but everything is good on my end."

"I appreciate that, homie. I'll hit you up later." We said our goodbyes, and I hung up the phone. A part of me wanted to call Janelle and hear her side, but the prideful part of me wouldn't let me do it. Instead of calling her, I called my sister.

"You dumb ass, nigga," she greeted with an attitude.

"The fuck wrong with you?"

"What's wrong with you?" she countered.

"Janelle is on the other line, telling me you broke up with her. The fuck is wrong with you, Shariq." I huffed because I knew she was about to take this girl's side without knowing why I broke it off with her.

"Man, I don't want to hear that. She couldn't wait to go out with the next nigga." I defended my actions.

"Did you know that the nigga was Kyren's father, and he was with them? Did you know that he knows all about you because all Kyren does is talk about your dumb ass? Then you let Mariah, of all people, get in your head. When has she ever looked out for your best interest?" She kept fussing like she

89

was my damn mama and I let her. She was right. I didn't even give Janelle the benefit of the doubt to listen to her, and she asked me to let her explain.

"Can you merge us?" I begged.

"She hung up as soon as I said it was you calling. She also said not to call for you," she informed.

"I can just call myself."

"You can try, but you should know that she has you blocked." I dropped my head because I knew that I fucked up and I didn't know what I was going to do about it.

"Shay, can you just call her for me, please?"

"I'm not doing that. You should've listened to the girl from the beginning," she chastised.

"Who's side are you on?" I asked her.

"The side of right and right now, that's not you." She was right. I needed to take my 'L' like a man and suck the shit up.

"Aight, man. If you talk to her, can you just let her know I'm sorry?"

"I got you, fathead. I love you."

"I love you, too, sis." I hung up the phone with Shay and tried calling Janelle back myself, and sure enough, she had me blocked. Shaking my head, I put my phone up and laid my ass down to take a nap. I didn't know how I was going to fix this shit, but I had to figure it out.

Chapter Ten

Shariq

Four months later...

I was getting released today, and no one knew but Shay. I asked her to keep it a secret so I could pop up on everybody, mainly Janelle. I missed that damn girl. She really shut me out. I got her address from Shay so I could write her and send her some shit and everything that I sent got fuckin' returned. She wouldn't accept shit from Shay and Cruz, either. The only thing that she had no control over was the money that I had deposited into her account, but she told Shay to let me know that she wasn't touching it and she'll have it all when I got home. I didn't want that shit back, but I would let her think she was doing something. I was getting released early because typical Duval County was getting overcrowded, and I've been on my best behavior minus the incident with Mooney's bitch ass. As I was being processed out, I couldn't help but think about Janelle. I needed to lay my eyes on her first before I did anything else, but I had to see my daughter first. It took them forever to process me out, but when they did, Shay was outside waiting for me. I noticed her car and went straight to it. I let myself in and was met with her big ass smile.

"Nigga, did you eat the weights?" she teased.

"Nah, but I had to release all that tension some kind of way since my girl wasn't fuckin' with me." I saw her face change when I mentioned Janelle.

"Wassup? I saw that look on your face when I mentioned her name."

"Ain't nothing up, but you need to go see her."

"I plan on it, but I'm going to see my daughter first. Did you get rid of that other car?" I asked.

"You know I did. Your new one is at your house." I nodded and laid my head back on the headrest. I had to get my mind right in order to see my daughter again and my girl. I listened as she told me that she was still spending time with Kyren, and that made me hopeful that she hadn't cut me off completely.

"They had a great season and Ray got him on his friend's basketball team," she informed me.

"I got home just in time to start the season. It's good that they're in the same league, so I can make it to him and Riah's games."

"Yep. I know she can't wait to see you. It was hard not keeping her home today, but I didn't want to ruin the surprise."

"I appreciate that, sis. Does Janelle have any clients today?" I asked.

"No, she stopped taking clients on Wednesdays and the weekends."

"Can she afford to do that?"

"She can. Sis' can take off a month if she wants to." I nodded because I was genuinely happy for her. We pulled up to my house and after I told her I would go see Ma after I checked in on my other girls.

Going inside of my house, I knew Shay had been here to clean up and restock my refrigerator. I went straight to my bedroom and stripped out of the jail issued sweats and got straight into the shower. I had one of the boys in the quad hook me up with a haircut and shave so I could save time by not going to the barbershop. I took my time in the shower because this was one of the main luxuries that I missed. Once I was done, I got dressed in a tan Jordan hoodie with white lines, adoring it along with the matching sweatpants. I paired the outfit with the matching retro Jordan 5s and hat. After spraying my signature cologne, I was back out the door and headed to my baby mama's house. I was going to chill there until my baby girl got home. I didn't want to risk getting caught up doing anything else before I laid eyes on her. Hopefully, Mariah didn't piss me off to where I didn't have a choice but to leave.

The ride to her house was quiet since I was lost in my thoughts. I wanted to get my mind right before being around her because this girl was literally a pain in my ass. It took all of thirty-five minutes to get to her house from mine. I was thankful that traffic was light because 295 was always a muthafucka to navigate through. When I pulled into the yard, I saw Cruz' car. Trying not to think the worse, I parked my car and got out. I knocked on the door and waited for Mariah to bring her ass to the door. When she did, I immediately saw red. This bitch was in her fuckin' underwear and a thin ass robe.

"Fr-Shariq, what are you doing out?" she asked. I mugged her ass and pushed her out of my way, barging into the house.

"The fuck that nigga at?" I growled. Before she could answer, my so-called friend emerged from the back shirtless with just a pair of basketball shorts and socks on.

"Frost?" he said, like he saw a ghost. I didn't even respond to his ass. I stepped to him and rocked his shit with two quick jabs to his face.

"Shariq!" I heard Mariah yell my name.

"Frost, man. I was going to tell you," Cruz said through a bloody lip.

"You was gon' tell me? It shouldn't be shit to tell!" My voice roared.

"Shariq! Stop it! Why do you even care? You don't want me and your lil' girlfriend pregnant now, so you can leave me and my business alone." I froze when she said Janelle was pregnant.

"The fuck did you just say? Who's pregnant?" I

asked for clarity.

"Oh, you didn't know?" she smirked. "Must not be yours then." I didn't even stay to let her say that shit to my face. I let her get in my head once before but not this time.

"My daughter better be in place when I get back. I wouldn't test me if I were you," was all I said before I left her house and sped to Janelle's. I was glad that I got the address from Shay because I knew if I called, she would ignore me, and I didn't need that right now. If she was indeed pregnant, she might as well get over being mad because wasn't no way out of this shit now.

I pulled into her condo complex and navigated my way to her unit. When I pulled up, I saw an Infinite SUV parked beside the empty guest spot. I pulled into the guest space and hightailed it to her door. I rang the bell and waited for her to open the door. I heard the locks turn and then she snatched the door open. Her face was balled up as she stared at me, but I couldn't tear my eyes away from her round belly that was barely covered by her tank top and spandex shorts. I remembered we were standing in the door and pushed her back slightly as I shut the door behind me.

"You always answer the door half naked?" I asked.

"I thought it was my nigga," she snapped back, trying to walk away.

"Don't play wit' me, shorty." I gripped her arm lightly to keep her from walking away.

"Let me go," her husky voice growled, causing my dick to stir.

"Why didn't you tell me?" I asked.

"Tell you for what? You called me a hoe, remember?" She cocked her head to the side.

"Baby, I didn't call you a hoe. I was just upset."

"And you took the word of your triflin' ass baby mama over mine. She's the one you should've been worried about and not me." She turned to walk off and this time I let her, but followed close behind.

"I know," I said as I followed her to her bedroom. I looked around and sighed when it didn't look like another nigga lived here, or even been here for that matter.

"What you mean, you know?"

"I mean just what I said." I told her what happened when I went over there, and she just looked at me.

"Look, I would've come here first, but I wanted to see my daughter before anyone else." She just looked at me.

"Unlike you, Shariq. I understand the importance of being a parent and I know that comes with being around the other parent." She shot back. I attempted to pull her into my lap at first, but she hesitated. I gave her a pleading look, and she finally gave in.

"Look, baby. I'm sorry for jumping to conclusions about what she told me. I should've given you the opportunity to tell me for myself, but I was too prideful. I truly apologize for that shit. I was literally sick thinking about you wit' another nigga." I confessed.

"Good. You should've been. Here I am, big and pregnant, and I couldn't even share it with you." She pouted.

"You could've, but you wanted to be stubborn and not do it."

"Do you blame me? I wasn't about to be stressed because of you telling me that my baby wasn't yours. When I had sex with you, I hadn't had sex with anyone for a year. After I had sex with you, I haven't had sex with anyone else," she admitted.

"Yo' ass better not had." I rubbed her stomach.

"You know what we're having?"

"Yeah. I got you a gift that I was going to send to you, eventually. Hold on, let me get it." Reluctantly, I let her up and watched as she waddled into her closet and came back with a box. She handed it to me, and I gave her one last look before I opened it. Inside was a white t-shirt that said, 'Original Version' and a smaller one that said, 'Edited Version'. I looked at her and she was smiling at me.

"You giving me a Junior?" She nodded.

"Damn, shorty. Come here." I moved the box out of the way and pulled her back into my lap. I cupped the sides of her face and said, "thank you."

"For what?"

"For keeping my baby even when I was acting like a dumb ass nigga. Thank you for that." I kissed her lips, but she deepened it. I was thrown off a little, but I damn sure wasn't backing down.

Breaking the kiss, I took kicked my shoes off and pulled off my sweatshirt. I gently lifted her off my lap and laid her down on the bed. I lowered my lips to her stomach and placed a kiss on it before caressing it. I felt my boy kick and couldn't help the smile that spread across my face.

"Lil' nigga, already strong as hell." My chest swelled with pride.

"Shariq?" she called out to me.

"Wassup, baby?"

"Fuck me." Her voice low and demanding.

"Shit, say less, mama." I stripped out of my clothes and discarded hers before I eased my way into what I knew would be my new home. This was definitely the welcome home that I needed.

Chapter Eleven

Janelle

Three months later...

The day Shariq got out of jail caught me completely by surprise. I knew he had two months left but low and behold, my baby daddy popped up on me looking good as hell with his grill in his mouth and his chains around his neck. I wanted to jump on him right in the doorway, but I quickly remembered that I was mad at his ass. After I told him about our son, he fucked me senseless before volunteering to go pick up Kyren. I already had his name on his list, along with his sister, mother, and uncle, so all he had to do was show his ID. He told me he would go and get Shariah too, so he could spend time with them. He did just that and I enjoyed a much needed nap. That was three months ago, and today we were getting ready for our baby shower. Shay was hosting, but of course, Lex came down to help her. I was so happy to have her here with me. She visited twice since I found out I was pregnant, but it was different to have her here now that Shariq was home. They walked on the phone and over FaceTime but never met in person.

Speaking of home, he moved me and Kyren into his house. Kyren loved it because it was closer to the beach. I was hesitant at first, but he assured me that no other woman hasn't lived or slept there outside of Shay and his mama. He was somewhere with Kyren while I got ready for today's festivities. This was also his birthday weekend, so we would be busy tomorrow as well. It was mid-February, so I had on a pair of white tights with a long, long-sleeved tunic that had slits on the side. I paired my outfit with a pair of blue thigh high flat boots. My hair was freshly cut, curled and styled, and my makeup was light. I was finally ready to go to celebrate with my new family. As I made my way down the stairs, Shariq met me at the bottom.

"Mama, why didn't you call me to come help you? You know I don't like you going up and down these stairs by yourself, baby." He held his hand out to assist me coming down the last few steps.

"Yeah, Ma. You know better." Kyren added his two cents in. He was Shariq's clone, so I didn't know what I would do when the new baby got here.

"Ky, so you just going to abandon your mama like that?" I feigned hurt.

"Don't worry, Nellie. You still got me." Shariah came to my rescue as always. She was spending more time with us since Cruz and Mariah were now in a relationship and having their own baby. I tried to get Shariq to hash things out with him, but he wasn't hearing it. He assured me that it had nothing to do with Mariah, but of how he went by doing things. He said he could never trust a nigga like that and after thinking about it, I agreed.

"That's right, baby girl. Don't let them gang up on me." I smirked at Shariq.

He pulled me into his body and whispered in my ear and said, "I want you to pop that same shit when we get back home tonight." He returned the smirk, followed by a hard smack on my butt.

"Sis, we gon' have to wear our headphones tonight," Kyren whispered to Shariah, or at least he thought. Shariq thought that was the funniest thing in the world, and I was mortified.

"Aye, y'all get y'all lil' nosy asses in the car. Y'all staying wit' ya nana tonight." He faked fussed.

"Good. She lets us eat brownies and ice cream for the night." Kyren shrugged. We could only shake our heads because it was no use in arguing with him.

After he helped me into his truck. We headed toward the venue. When we pulled up, there were blue, silver, and black balloons everywhere. The kids ran inside as Shariq came to help me out.

"If all this is going on outside, I could just imagine what's going on, on the inside." He ushered me into the venue, and everyone started clapping and cheering when we made it inside. Shay and Lex had it decorated in blue, silver and black. Pictures of the maternity shoot Shariq and I did when he came home were plastered over the walls. Everything was so beautiful. I was trying to hold my tears at bay, but it wasn't any use.

"I knew your big crybaby ass was gon' cry." Shariq chuckled as he lightly wiped my tears, careful not to mess up my makeup.

"Shut up." I shoved him.

"You look gorgeous, sis," Shay said as she approached me.

"Thank you. I feel like a blimp, though."

"You're a sexy ass blimp, though." Shariq kissed me and grabbed my butt.

"I bet that's how you got pregnant in the first place." I froze when I heard her voice. Quickly, I whipped my head around and saw my mother standing there in her uniform. I couldn't stop the tears now if I wanted to.

"Mommy!" I shrieked, jumping up and down like a big kid.

"Aye, I know you're happy, but stop all that before you shake my boy up." Shariq warned.

I went to my mother and gave her a big hug.

"Why didn't you tell me you were coming?" I asked.

"Then it would ruin the surprise. Look at you. You weren't this big with Ky. Where is he, anyway?" As if that was hie que, he came over to where we were and when he saw my mother, he took off and jumped on her.

"Grandma!" He squeezed her tightly.

"Oh, wow. You've gotten so big. Look at you." She goaded.

We shared more hugs and did introductions before we opened our gifts. A lot of my clients showed up, even the ones from Georgia and South Florida. Everything was perfect, even up until my water broke.

"Oh," I gasped, causing Shariq to give me his attention.

"What's wrong?" His eyes were searching me frantically.

"My...my water broke," I cried.

"What? Oh, shit." He jumped up and stood in front of me. "Uhm, can you stand up?" he asked. I nodded my head, and he helped me stand.

"This is definitely Shariq's baby. How are you going to ruin your own baby shower?" Shay fussed.

"Aye, chill out. My boy can do what he wants," Shariq said as he ushered me outside.

"Baby, are you having any pains yet?"

"No." I breathed out.

He helped me inside of the truck and broke every speed limit to get me to the hospital. When we arrived, he ushered straight inside and that's when my first contraction hit, causing me to buckle over in pain.

"Ahh!" I screamed.

"Aye! Y'all hurry up!" I heard him yell.

Moments later, I staff of nurses came into view and got to work. They rushed me to a room where they were getting me ready for delivery. I heard them say that my doctor was on the way, and that eased my anxiety a little bit.

I didn't want a stranger delivering my baby.

Chapter Twelve

Shariq

Ain't this some shit. We were enjoying our family while we prepared to welcome our baby boy. I guess he heard all the excitement and decided to make his grand entrance. Janelle had been in labor for six hours, and she was growing restless. My boy was already taking her through it, and he hadn't even made it here yet.

"Baby, you're doing so good." I coached, kissing her head.

"This baby is stubborn as hell. I wonder where he got that from?" She cut her eyes at me.

"Chill out. It's not that bad." She shot me a look when I said that. I didn't mean to upset her, so I tried my best to soothe things over. She was getting tired and so was I, but I wasn't about to miss this shit for the world.

The doctor came in and checked her. This time, she told her it was time for her to start pushing. A nurse took me out of the room to get cleaned up and I made a detour to let the family know that it was showtime. When I made it back into the room, they already had her legs up in those stirrup things and she was propped up. I leaned down and kissed her forehead.

"I love you, baby."

"I love you, too." She cried.

"Okay, Janelle. When you feel the next contraction, I need you to give me a big push so we can get this little guy here. Okay?" Janelle responded with a nod and when the next contraction hit, she squeezed my hand hard as fuck.

"Ahhh!" She screamed as she pushed with all her might.

"You're doing good, mama. I'm so proud of you," I praised. She dropped her head back on the pillow and was breathing hard. I leaned over and kissed her lips, and she gave me a weak smile.

"Okay. That was good. If you can give me one more like that, we can get his head out," the doctor said.

"He has your big ass head," my baby snapped at me.

All I said was, "I know, baby."

The next contraction hit, and she pushed with all her might. Seconds later, I heard my son's loud cries pierce my eyes. Tears immediately sprang to my eyes.

"Somebody had some strong lungs," the doctor announced.

"That's my boy," I stated proudly.

The doctor instructed Janelle to give her one last push and my son was finally here. His cries were strong and loud, making my chest swell with pride.

"Time of birth, 12:16 AM." The nurse announced the time and Janelle looked at me and said, "Happy Birthday." I smiled after realizing my son shared the same birthday with me. This was the best birthday I ever had.

"Thank you, baby. Thank you for my son and for answering the phone." I smirked.

The End!!

Note From Author

I hope you enjoyed this short story about Shariq and Janelle's love story. The idea came to me after I had a call from an actual inmate who dialed the wrong number looking for his family. I don't know what his fate was but hopefully it ended happy, like Shariq and Janelle's

Made in United States
Orlando, FL
02 December 2024

54886061R00065